William Filley

Life and Adventures of William Filley

Who was Stolen from His Home in Jackson, Mich., by the Indians

William Filley

Life and Adventures of William Filley
Who was Stolen from His Home in Jackson, Mich., by the Indians

ISBN/EAN: 9783337055790

Printed in Europe, USA, Canada, Australia, Japan

Cover: Foto ©Raphael Reischuk / pixelio.de

More available books at **www.hansebooks.com**

LIFE AND ADVENTURES

OF

WILLIAM FILLEY,

WHO WAS

STOLEN FROM HIS HOME

IN

JACKSON, MICH., BY THE INDIANS,

August 3d, 1837,

AND HIS

SAFE RETURN FROM CAPTIVITY,

October 19, 1866.

AFTER AN ABSENCE OF 29 YEARS.

CHICAGO:
PUBLISHED BY FILLEY & BALLARD.
......
1867.

DEDICATION.

THE AUTHOR, in presenting this (2d) Edition to a more than generous public, MOST RESPECTFULLY Dedicates this work to that NOBLE BAND of early pioneers of Michigan, whose arduous and untiring efforts in the great search, and common sympathies for the "LONG LOST JACKSON BOY," and heart broken parents, deserve the highest mark of affection, and lasting remembrance.

PREFACE.

In presenting this work to the public, we feel that we are giving a statement of facts which are not only of great interest, but which will, in time, become portions of the Indian history of the distant West. The affidavits and certificates which are introductory to the Indian Boy's own narrative, are *bona fide*, the parties making them being respectable and reliable people.

We have been particular in giving all possible evidence as to the identity of the long lost boy, that no possible doubt may remain; but feeling that a better idea can be obtained from his own story, have not attempted to minutely describe many of the scenes through which he passed. We, therefore, in the following pages, submit the evidence and the narrative.

CONTENTS

CHAPTER IV.

CHAPTER V.

CHAPTER VI.

CHAPTER VII.

CHAPTER VIII.

CHAPTER IX.

CHAPTER X.

CONCLUSION

THE SONG OF "THE LAKE OE THE WHITE CANOE."

MARY MOUNT.

INTRODUCTION.

INTRODUCTION.

MRS. MOUNT'S CERTIFICATE.

I hereby certify that I am the mother of Mary Mount, in whose charge William Filley was placed at the time he was lost, and that I am now seventy-two years of age.

Twenty-nine years ago the third day of August last, William Filley accompanied my daughter Mary to a swamp a short distance from my residence, for the purpose of gathering whortleberries. I remember well the peculiar style of his dress, and that some friendly hand had placed in the button-hole of his little coat some pinks; he had with him a piece of paper with writing upon it, which I learned he had obtained from his Aunt Fitch. William and my daughter Mary left my house a short time after twelve o'clock of said third day of August. We endeavored to persuade the little fellow not to go, fearing that he would be bitten by the snakes which infested that part of the country. Our entreaties were in vain, and the boy went along. After William and Mary had been absent a few hours, Mary returned to our house and made inquiries for William. Of course he had not returned, and our fears were excited, believing that he had met with some untimely fate. I made inquiries of my daughter about what had become of the boy, and the only explanation which she could give was that he had become weary and wanted to go home ; that she had led him to a beaten track which led to our house, and that this was the last time she had seen him. Immediately we made a, thorough search but could find no trace of him; the neighborhood was aroused and diligent work commenced. That night fires were built for two reasons : First, believing that the lost boy would see them ; and secondly, that the light would aid us in our search. Fortunately, there were good brush and log heaps near the swamp, which burned all night.

About two miles in a westerly course, lived a family named Hamilton, who reported that about ten or eleven o'clock of that night, they heard a strange noise resembling the stifled cry of a child; and near this place, in the oak openings, was found the identical piece of letter paper which I have heretofore mentioned. The search was continued, and the crowd gathered near the place where this paper was found. Arrangements were immediately made as to the disposition of the force : The crowd formed a circle, enclosing a large space of country, and each man walked so near his comrade that he could touch his person., In many places in the swamp the men crept upon their hands and knees, turning over the moss and other substances which they found in their way. As the circle shortened in distance, and on coming near together,

GREAT SEARCH FOR THE BODY OF THE LOST BOY
IN FITCH'S LAKE, AND IN THE VICINITY OF MRS. MOUNT'S HOUSE, AUGUST 4, 1837.

they found three bears and several deer which they allowed to escape, not deeming it proper to discharge fire-arms, as this was the signal agreed upon if the child should be found. For a time attention was drawn from the Indian trails and camping ground, owing to a report put in circulation by one Albert Crandall, who had succeeded in creating a suspicion that the child had met with some accident, and had been foully dealt with by my daughter Mary. Consequently a thorough search was made in and around our premises and house, and some person broke open our chests and broke into the tills. The ash-heaps were turned over for the purpose of finding the bones of the child, if possible, and every spot was searched and re-searched, in vain by hundreds of men. I have no doubt that there were at least eight hundred persons at this time about our premises.

Our house was located upon the banks of Fitch's lake, a beautiful sheet of water, covering about six hundred and forty acres of land. This lake was dragged during the day time, and at night was searched with the aid of torchlights and small rafts, instead of boats, many persons wading in from the shore.

Twenty-nine years have passed away since the memorable day when William Filley left our then quiet home. Many of the early settlers of Jackson county are dead. I am thankful that I have been spared to see that boy again, and to have the cloud of suspicion removed which hung over our heads. I have no doubt of the identity of the person whose narrative is contained in this book. He is now in the prime of manhood. May he long survive, and be the staff of his aged father, and live in near communion with that Great Spirit who has thus far been his guide in his wanderings with the red men of the forest.

LYDIA MOUNT.

GRANDISON FILLEY'S CERTIFICATE.

JACKSON, November 5, 1866.

I hereby certify that I am the uncle of William Filley, and that I knew him from his birth, until he was stolen by the Indians on the third day of August, 1837, he then being five years, one month, and one day old. At the age of two years William was left with me at Bloomfield, in the State of Connecticut.

At that time Ammi Filley, his father, was in Michigan, and his mother was with her father, Captain William Marvin, in the State of Massachusetts. At Elijah Filley's house, in the State of Connecticut, we were picking apples, late in the fall. William had on an old coat with long sleeves, somewhat troublesome in picking up fruit, I took out my pocket knife and in cutting them off shorter, I accidentally cut his thumb, on his left hand, nearly off. I doubled up his hand, drew down the sleeve, and told him to keep his hand shut. As I drew the knife across the sleeve the boy stuck out his thumb, and I cut it diagonally from joint to joint.

I also certify, that I have seen, at different times from the 19th day of October, 1866, until the present date, a man purporting to be William Filley, the long lost boy. From every feature, motion, and personal appearance, I should judge him to be the same one; he has the same large cut-scar on his left thumb, and it shows as plain as it did thirty years ago. I am positive upon this point, and recollect well the shape of the wound and scar.

GRANDISON FILLEY.

· CERTIFICATES BY CITIZENS OF JACKSON.

We, the undersigned residents of the City of Jackson, and State of Michigan, hereby certify that we were citizens of said township in the year A. D. 1837, and that on and after the third day of August, in that year, we went in person, with many hundreds and thousands of others, in fruitless search for William Filley, the subject of this history, then a boy of five years of age, supposed to have been murdered, or stolen from his parents by the Pottawatamies, a tribe of Indians that shortly afterwards moved from this State to the far West; that the boy's father now survives, and recognizes his long lost son, by his appearance, and by a cut-scar on his thumb, after an absence of twenty-nine years and more, spent in the Rocky Mountains.

Hon. DAN'L B. HIBBARD,
ALBERT FOSTER, Esq.,
WILLIAM PAGE, Esq.,
LEWIS BASCOM, Esq.,
M. E. DWYER, Esq.,
ISAAC PETERSON, Esq.,
T. N. HENDERSON, Esq.,
S. P. HENDERSON, Esq,
JAMES A. DYER, J. P.,
W. H. MONROE, Esq.,
B. F. EGGLESTON, Esq.,
S. W. STOWELL, Esq.,
PATTON MORRISON, Esq.,
D. T. DURAND, Esq.,
GEO. FERGUSON, Esq.,
MARCUS WAKEMAN, Esq.,
H. ANSON, Esq.,
SAM'L PETERSON, Esq.,
DAVID MARKHAM, Esq.,

Hon. WM. R. DELAND,
W. D. THOMPSON, Banker,
JAMES WELCH, Esq.,
F. FARRAND, Esq.,
ISAAC SNYDER, Esq.,
B. C. HATCH, Esq.,
L. SNYDER, Jr.,
C. R. HARRINGTON, Esq.,
THOS. VREELAND, Esq.,
WARREN MOULTON, Esq.,
CYRUS HODGKIN, Esq.,
WM. P. WORDEN, Esq.,
C. P. RUSSELL, Esq.,
ALDEN HEWETT, Esq.,
Hon. A. H. DELAMATER,
W. KNICKERBOCKER, Esq.,
J. W. PRUE, Esq.,
N. E. ALLEN, Esq.

We, the undersigned, citizens of the City of Jackson, and State of Michigan, hereby certify that we are well acquainted with the fact of William Filley being stolen by the Indians, and of his return from his long captivity.

Hon. M. A. McNoughton,   Hon. D. Fisher,

J. E. Bebe, Assessor 3d Dis-   Norman Allen, Esq.,

    trict, Michigan,   W. Greg, Esq.,

E. B. Brigham, Esq.,   T. D. Budington, Esq.,

A. I. Hobort, Esq.,   H. Wakeman, Esq.

C. Warriner, Esq.,

MR. LYONS' CERTIFICATE.

Jackson, November 20th, 1866.

I hereby certify that I am a son of Dea. Lyons, of East Mendon, Monroe County, New York; I am thirty-five years of age, and have lived most of the past sixteen years with different Indian tribes in the far West. I spent one month (about the time of the war with Mexico,) with the Pottawattamies, a tribe that had moved a few years previous to that time from the State of Michigan. I also was with said tribe about six weeks in the year 1860, on the Missouri bottoms, where the river Platte runs through, and while there I learned from the tribe that a white child had been stolen years before from Jackson County, Michigan.

I am now visiting in the city of Jackson, Michigan, where I shall remain for a few days with my friends and relatives, and have learned that a man has returned from the Rocky Mountains, and is recognized by his father and relatives as the boy that was supposed to have been stolen from his parents in 1837. I also certify that in the spring of 1849, at the mouth of Feather River, near where now is the city of Marysville, I saw a white boy, apparently about seventeen or eighteen years of age, on his way to school with two Indian chiefs. One, the Big Crow Chief, told me they were going to leave him at school in San Francisco, to learn the English language. I little thought that I should ever have an opportunity of conversing with him face to face about the Rocky Mountains, or talk Spanish and Indian with him at the home of his relatives.

DANIEL M. LYONS.

STATEMENT OF AMMI FILLEY, THE FATHER OF WILLIAM FILLEY.

At the request of several persons who are conversant with the important facts relative to the loss of my son in the summer of 1837, I have consented to make the following statement: In the month of October last, while residing with one of my sons in the State of Illinois, I received a telegram from the city of Jackson, requesting my return for the purpose of meeting my son, William Filley, whose strange and simple story is told in this book. I immediately departed for that city, and on arriving met with a person whom I believe is my long lost son—my eldest one, and the object of my search for many, many years. Although many persons had suggested the probability that my son had been foully dealt with, I had a vague idea that he had been taken off by some of the Indian tribes who at an early day were wander-ing in our woods in Michigan. My paternal affection dic-tated to me that it was my duty to search among the red men for my lost son. I gave up my business and became a wanderer among the Indians. I led a roving life for many years, and during that time visited the tribes of Indians in Michigan, Ohio, Canada, and other portions of the country. This trouble unsettled my plans of life and deprived me of that peace of mind which all persons wish to enjoy. I am fifty-nine years old and am travelling down the hill of life, and feel as if my cup of happiness was filled, the great object of my ambition accomplished. I have found my lost son. I sincerely thank my friends who have rendered me so much assistance and who have sympathized with me in my affliction. May they live long and enjoy that happiness which belongs to a well-ordered life.

AMMI FILLEY.

THE ABDUCTION.

A CHILD IS LOST.

Oh, KINSMEN, neighbors, friends, our child is lost!
The night is falling; help, for love of God!
In fruitless search the fields we've trod,
And, vainly, every trail and path we've crossed.
The mother's heart is breaking; friends take pity—
Forth, quickly forth, and scour the darkening woods.
A child is lost! a tiny, tottering one,
Whose age is scarcely reckoned yet by years;
Whose feet but little time have learned to run;
Whose words are simple words, in accent broken.
He scarce can tell his name, nor where he dwells,
Or else his words so modestly are spoken
That strangers cannot understand the tale he tells.
The slow and solemn clock tolls forth eleven;
Again it strikes, 'tis midnight now!   How fearfully the
            hour
Trembles upon the calm, quiescent air
As many a wearied seeker homeward speeds,
To bid the mourning mother trust in Heaven,
And, on her couch, to seek the rest she needs.

Oh! can I sleep when he is still unfound—
A helpless lamb that's wander'd from the fold;
And he, perhaps, is crying, tired, and hungry,
Or sleeps, to die, upon the cold, cold ground?
How can I rest, when I, perchance, shall see
No more the child whom God once gave to me?
Comfort me, kind neighbors, leave me not forlorn;
Is there no hope?   Is life henceforth to be
Of joy, and peace, and pleasant memories shorn?
Pity me, friends, in mine extremity.

PARTICULARS OF THE LOSS OF WILLIAM FILLEY.

There are many interesting incidents connected with the life of this individual that are worthy of a place in "American History."

Ammi Filley, father of William, removed from Hartford County, Connecticut, in the year 1833, to the oak openings of Michigan, and located with his family in the township of Jackson, then a wilderness. By industry and economy he soon became the possessor of a good farm. Although surrounded by Indian tribes they had no fear, as all were apparently friendly.

It was on the third day of August, A. D. 1837, that William Filley, then a child of the tender age of five years, one month and one day, went out to a swamp near by with a hired girl by the name of Mary Mount, to gather berries. The swamp was between the house of Mr. Filley and the dwelling of Mr. Mount, the father of the girl. After picking berries for a time, little William expressed a wish to go home. Whereupon the girl led him to the trail and pointed out the way to her father's house, which was in sight. Not doubting, as the house was in plain sight, only a few rods distant, that the little fellow would reach it in perfect safety, she returned to the swamp.

After completing her supply of berries, she went to the house of her father, and found, to her astonishment, as well as to that of her family, that the little boy put in her charge had not returned; neither had he been to the home of his parents. Whereupon an alarm was immediately given and all the inhabitants commenced a most diligent search for the lost child, and continued their untiring efforts by day and night for weeks. Every pond and stream was dragged and

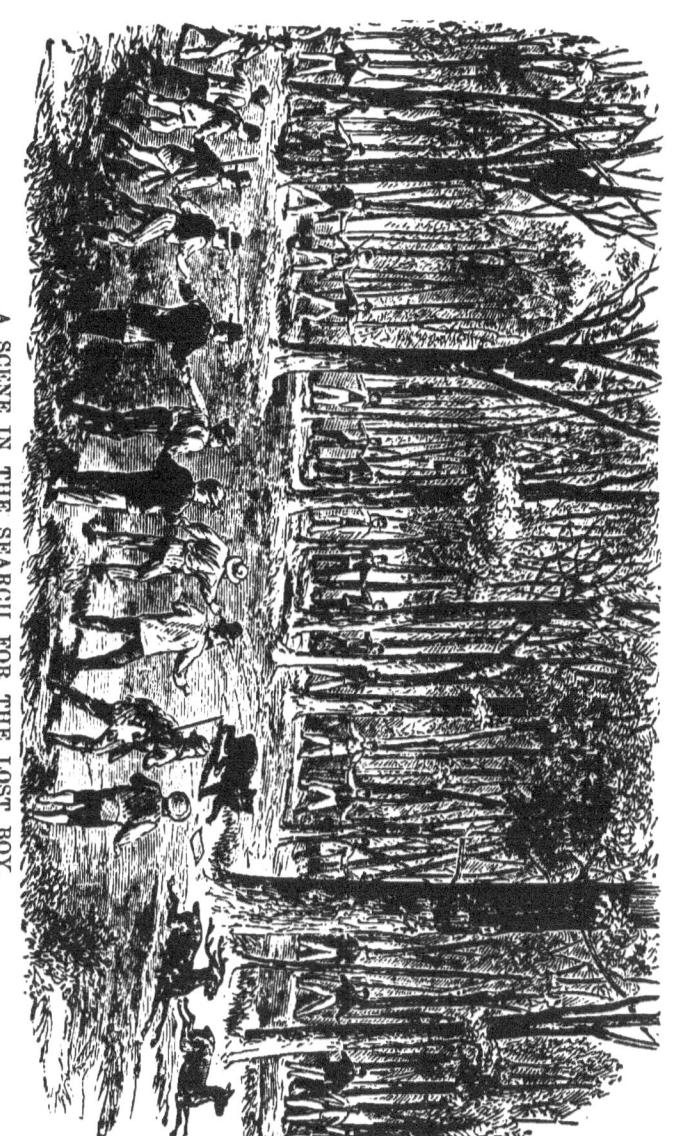

A SCENE IN THE SEARCH FOR THE LOST BOY.

The identical spot where the paper was found, as referred to in Mrs. Mount's certificate.—From a photograph.

examined, and every rod of ground scrutinized to an extent of more than twenty miles around.

As an inducement to continue the search, notice of the event was given in the papers, and large rewards offered for the recovery of the child, either dead or alive. Gold and silver was offered to the different Indian tribes in large sums by disinterested persons.

Mr. Filley's voice was heard late at night and early in the morning calling, William! William! That familiar name was echoed from lake to lake, and from Green Bay to Ohio! The distracted father went in person all over the wilds of Michigan, Wisconsin, and Iowa, visiting many tribes of Indians.

> All along the Grand River
> And adown the shady glen,
> On the hill and in the valley,
> Were the graves of dusky men.

Fears were entertained that the Indians were not well pleased with the way the pale faces had ploughed up their burying grounds, and that in the wilds of some inhospitable region, where foot of white man had never trod, the boy had fallen a sacrifice to the vengeance of some infuriated savage.

No discovery could the father make and no tidings learn. Returning in sorrow to his family, all were heart-broken, as the last ray of hope was extinguished. The fond parents gave up their firstborn child as forever lost.

> Of purest joy, of life itself,
> 'Twere sad, indeed, to say
> How much of all, lost William!
> Has passed with thee away.

Can you imagine a sadder scene? Such agony of afflic- tion seldom falls to the lot of man. If the shaft of death had

2

smitten down this their darling boy, and they had passed through the funeral solemnities and seen him laid in the grave of their own church-yard, time would have tempered their grief and mitigated the anguish of their bereavement; but the painful suspense, the awful uncertainty that hung over his fate was an abiding sorrow which time would not soften, and earth had no balm to heal. Time rolled on, but William was not forgotten.

The mournful event, with its aggravating circumstances, was a corroding canker on the comforts of the family, causing the fatal disease which seized the Christian mother as she went down in sorrow to an untimely grave. "Imagination portrays the Guardian Angel, suspended equi-distant between earth and the blue azure of Heaven, with her wings folded." The tear was on her cheek as she looked down upon the pitiful scene of the mother, gazing on each fond face as they clustered around her bedside. But one was not—her first-born! The dying mother whispers, "Where is he?" The wild winds in and around that dismal swamp, with their sepulchral voice, take up the dirge and echo, "Where, O! where is he?"

This worthy and beautiful woman was the oldest child of Captain William Marvin, a wealthy and very respectable citizen of East Granville, Hamden County, Massachusetts, after whom William was named.

Subsequent to the death of his wife, Mr. Filley visited the State of Connecticut, the place of his nativity. While there, by a miraculous course of events beyond the comprehension of human wisdom to fathom, a boy had been found in the possession of a party of Indians in the city of Albany and State of New York.

The circumstance being made known to the municipal authorities, the migrating party were arrested, and all measures taken to compel them to disclose the means by which they came in possession of the child. They were alternately flat-tered and threatened, but no disclosure could be obtained, and they seemed resolved to submit to any punishment rather than make communication by which the paternity of the child could be ascertained. They were therefore dis-charged, and the child humanely placed in the Orphan Asy-lum. From thence he was taken to Mr. Filley's friends in New England. He could tell of being in Green Bay, and of riding on a steamboat. He accompanied them in their wan-derings, and was used as a mendicant to supply himself with clothes and the wandering party with food, when their indo-lence prevented their obtaining it any other way. In the summer they made their peregrinations back and forth through Michigan and New York, sometimes visiting Con-necticut. In the winter they usually quartered themselves in wigwams in the vicinity of some village and lived on game. He remembered living near Detroit, Catskill, Hud-son, and Hillsdale. In their wanderings in summer and winter, he travelled barefoot, suffering in winter from cold, and at all times from hunger and fatigue. The kindness of his Indian sister, who, like a second Pocahontas, took un-wearied pains to mitigate his sufferings, made his captivity more endurable.

When all friends acquainted with the circumstances were rendering up grateful thanks to God, the author of all good, for this marvellous dispensation of His providence, the fol-lowing letter, from Mr. Collins, at that time Member of Con-gress, was received by the supposed grandfather of the child:

HILLSDALE, NEW YORK, February 13, 1845.
Captain WILLIAM MARVIN—

DEAR SIR: Having seen in the New York Evening Post,

a statement extracted from the Hartford City Times, in relation to the loss and finding of the child of Ammi Filley, of
Michigan, I read it with that interest which such a statement
would naturally excite; but at the conclusion, when the
names of the Indian family were mentioned, and the account
given that they had been for a time residents of this town, it
seemed to me, from what I had seen and heard, that Mr.
Filley must be mistaken as to the identity of the child. I
have since made further inquiries and am confirmed in the
opinion that Mr. Filley is mistaken. During the summer of
1838, an Indian family, including a white child, apparently
two or three years of age, took up their abode in a forest
about two miles from my place of residence. I often saw
them, and upon inquiring, I learned the name of the Indian
to be Paul, and that of the squaw to be Phebe. I understood
the child to be the son of the squaw and his father to be a
white man of the town of Copake, in this county. Those
Indians were living in this town in the summer of 1843, and
during the winter of 1844, and left in the spring of that year.

I am now told that those Indians resided in the towns of
Copake and Hillsdale most of the time from 1835 to the
spring of 1843. I am also told, by one of the most respectable men of Copake, that he frequently saw the child from the
period of a few months old, while it nursed from its mother,
and that the child did, for a short time, attend the District
School in the town of Copake.

I am also told that a physician, now residing in that town,
was present at the birth of the child. Disputes about the
paternity of the child, and intense domestic excitement pro-
duced on the occasion, have given to the matter a notoriety
that renders the subject of easy investigation, and the facts
of the case can be ascertained to a certainty. If Mr. Filley,

or his friends, should desire to inquire into this matter more minutely, I will either accompany them to see those better informed of the facts in this case, or I will get the statement from such persons, and will address them as may be desired.

It has been with much hesitancy, and upon deliberation, that I have taken this occasion to make to you this communication. It must be with great satisfaction that Mr. Filley is enabled to suppose that he has found his long lost son. It doubtless, too, is of much importance to the boy that Mr. Filley should remain under the delusion, (if it is such). If, too, the corroding wound in Mr. Filley's feelings has been healed by this discovery, it seems barbarous to tear it open and make it bleed again.

On the other hand, his actual child may be living. Under the impression that he may have found his son, he will stop further investigations and thereby prevent his own being found, which may yet, possibly be accomplished. His actual son, too, may hereafter present himself, and should he find his father's affections engrossed by another, he may not be able to prove his identity, and will find himself an alien in the home of his father. Under these views of the subject, I submit the matter to you. If you think it advisable to investigate the matter further I will give you all the assistance I am able. If you think it advisable to let Mr. Filley rest under his supposed discovery, or to communicate the discovery that you have, or that you may hereafter make, the subject is submitted to your discretion.

Most respectfully yours,

A. F. COLLINS.

MICHIGAN CENTRE, June 30, 1845.

MR. A. F. COLLINS—

DEAR SIR: Some time last month I visited Captain William Marvin, of Granville, Massachusetts, for the purpose of seeing a lost boy, supposed to be the son of Ammi Filley, of this county. Mr. Filley is a brother-in-law of mine, and we moved to this county some twelve years ago, and were near neighbors at the time of the loss of his boy, which occurred on the third day of August, 1837. The county was at that time new, and had Mr. Filley been an entire stranger, such an occurrence would, no doubt, have swelled my bosom with painful emotions, much more that parent being a relative and friend. While there, Captain Marvin showed me a letter, written by you, bearing date February 13, 1845, addressed to him. Judge, then, of my surprise (after reading the accounts in the papers, and hearing what was said by Mr. Filley's friends in Connecticut, whom I had just visited), on perusing your letter. Captain Marvin, as he is an old man, requested me to take the letter and either visit you or address you on my return. I am compelled to take the latter course; as I could not make it convenient to see you on my return from the East, I therefore take the liberty to address you, and as you kindly offered to make further investigations amongst those better acquainted with the facts, will you have the goodness to ascertain, First, if possible, in regard to the birth of the child, by the physician, or otherwise. Second, if those Indians were in Michigan in the summer of 1837. Third, if it was possible that the boy could have been six years old in the summer of 1838, when you say they were at Hillsdale, which would have been about the age of Mr. Filley's child. Fourth, please get a description of the boy's complexion, color of eyes, hair, &c., &c., and whether he had lost any of his toes, and if so, how many, and what ones; and finally, get such facts as you may think material, and write me as soon as convenient.

Mr. Filley is now in Michigan, and has no knowledge of the facts contained in your letter, nor do we think it advisable that he should know at present. As this was a favorite child, his loss has truly been a corroding wound. Mr. Filley has at times been partially deranged, and were we fully satisfied that it was not his child it would be imprudent, to say the least, to inform him of the fact at the present time. Although I am satisfied he has doubts about the identity of the child, yet, no one else acquainted with the facts, seems to have the least doubt except Captain Marvin and myself, for no other person has seen your letter. Will you have the goodness to write me as soon as convenient, and give me such information as you can obtain. Any trouble or expense that you may incur shall be promptly paid.

Truly yours,

ABEL F. FITCH.

Afterwards, Mr. Fitch went in person and procured a large amount of testimony, a portion of which is herewith annexed, showing clear and positive evidence that Mr. Collins was right in the supposition that this was not the child of Ammi Filley:

STATE OF NEW YORK, }
    Columbia County,   } ss.

John W. Dinehart, being duly sworn, deposes and says, that he resides in the town of Copake, County of Columbia, and State of New York; that he knew an Indian by the name of Paul Pry, and an Indian, or half-breed, woman, by the name of Phebe; that she was called his wife; that they resided in the town of Copake the winter of 1835 and 1836;

that they had with them a male child that appeared to be, and they said he was, about nine months old; that the child had lost a toe off one of his feet; that they said it had come by a string being around it, and that it was at last cut off; that they then left the place, and he don't recollect of seeing them again until in July, 1839; that they then had a little boy with them apparently about four years old, and from his complexion and the color of his hair, he has no doubt it was the same child they had with them when they left; that they then stayed in Copake awhile and went to the town of Hillsdale, adjoining Copake; that they were in Copake frequently till the summer of 1843; and that the boy attended the District School in that neighborhood.

JOHN W. DINEHART.

Subscribed, and sworn before)
  me, this 5th day of Septem- }
  ber, 1846.)

W. M. ELLIOTT,
Justice of the Peace, Columbia Co.

COLUMBIA COUNTY, ss.

Elizabeth Dinehart, being duly sworn, deposes and says: that she is the wife of John W. Dinehart; that the statements in the foregoing affidavit, made by him, are correct and true; that she has arrived at the dates stated in the foregoing affidavit from the records of the birth of her own children assisting her recollection.

her
ECLIMETA ⋈ DINEHART.
mark

Subscribed, and sworn before)
  me, this 5th day of Septem- }
  ber, 1846.)

W. M. ELLIOTT,
Justice of the Peace, Columbia Co.

COLUMBIA COUNTY, ss.

Christina Bain, being duly sworn, says: that she is the wife of Abraham Bain; that she resides in the town of Copake, in Columbia County; that she knew Paul Pry, and a woman, or a half-breed from appearance, that was said to be his wife; that they lived in Copake ten years ago; that they had a male child with them; that they left and returned again, about as stated in the affidavit of John W. Dinehart; that she thinks all the statements contained in that affidavit, as far as she can recollect, are correct.

her
CHRISTINA ⋈ BAIN
mark.

Subscribed, and sworn before
me, this 4th day of September, 1846. }

W. M. ELLIOTT,
Justice of the Peace Columbia Co.

COLUMBIA COUNTY, ss.

Loretta and Milton Bean, being duly sworn, each depose and say: that they agree in opinion with Christina Bain, of the affidavit of John W. Dinehart.

LORETTA BEAN,
MILTON BEAN.

Subscribed, and sworn before
me, this 5th day of September, 1846. }

W. M. ELLIOTT,
Justice of the Peace, Columbia Co.

COLUMBIA COUNTY, ss.

Polly Williams, being duly sworn, deposes, and says: that she resides in the town of Copake, in the County of Columbia; that she knew Paul Pry, an Indian, and a woman by the name of Phebe, a half-breed that was called his wife; that they had with them a male child, that suckled, and apparently less than a year old; think that this was about ten years ago; that the child had one toe that was nearly off, except a piece of skin; that its mother said it come by a string being around it; this deponent advised her to cut it off, which she declined doing, but afterwards, when she saw them, she had it cut off; she saw Paul, Phebe, and a little boy that had one toe off; that the eyes, hair and complexion of the boy were the same as that of the child she first saw with them.

POLLY WILLIAMS.

Subscribed, and sworn before ⎫
  me, this 5th day of Septem- ⎬
  ber, 1846. ⎭

W. M. ELLIOTT,
Justice of the Peace, Columbia Co.

Twenty-nine years have passed away. How marked the change! Many of the early settlers have disappeared from the stage of existence; another generation has succeeded them. The stalwart forms of the red men have left the beautiful banks of the Grand River for the hunting grounds. The pale-faces now occupy their possessions. The rattle of machinery and the whistle of the locomotive are heard instead of the shrill war-whoop; the wild oak openings have been turned into fruitful fields; the wigwams and rude huts have been changed into castles and new houses. Where now stands the flourishing and infant city of Jackson, marked by enterprise and prosperity so worthy our pride, destined to become the great Railroad Centre and Commercial Metropolis of the Lower Peninsula, were then the camping, hunting, and fishing grounds of the Pottawattamies.

In the early part of the month of October, 1866, the following letter was received by the Postmaster at Jackson:

'SIR:—Not knowing your name, but thinking that you would do me the favor to try and ascertain whether there is a man living in the city of Jackson, where you live, or anywhere else, by the name of Willey. I am his son. I was taken by the Indians about thirty years ago. Can you find any of the relatives of this Willey? All that I know about it is that my father's name is Willey, and' that I was taken from Michigan. This I was told by an Indian. Please to try and find out for me, and I will thank you, whether you find my father or not, as soon as you can make it convenient, as I want to see him or my relations.

Your humble serv't,
WILLIAM WILLEY.

COLDWATER, BRANCH CO., MICH., Sept. 28, 1866.

This letter, on account of its not being deemed by the Postmaster as of much consequence, was laid aside for several days. In a conversation held with the Hon. Daniel B. Hibbard, the Postmaster made the statement that he had received such a letter. As Mr. Hibbard was familiar with the fact of the loss of the boy William Filley, and presuming that the name of the writer was Filley instead of Willey, of course his curiosity was excited, and, consequently, the Postmaster was requested to make a search for it. A search was made, and the letter (of which the above is a copy) was found.

The author was immediately informed of the receipt of the foregoing letter, and, as soon as possible, commenced an investigation into the facts. Making a visit to Branch County, he learned that such a person had been there, but could not find him. A brother of William Filley, Elijah Filley, who then resided in Oil City, Pennsylvania, was telegraphed to, and went to Branch County, for the purpose of finding his brother if possible. While he was engaged in the search, the long lost boy, on the 19th of October, 1866, appeared in the city of Jackson, and received the welcome and embraces of a large number of friends and relatives, many of whom, years ago, had searched in vain for him.

The author was present at the time of the receipt of the telegram by the aged father, in Illinois, announcing the arrival of William, and witnessed the paternal affection manifested on that occasion. He immediately left for the city of Jackson, where he met and readily recognized his son, notwithstanding the great change which had taken place during an absence of twenty-nine years.

Time and exposure had somewhat obliterated the fair features of his youth. His personal appearance is the counterpart of his father. His complexion, age, and the color of his eyes and hair, and all his prominent characteristics are identical with those of the lost child. And, upon appealing to the well-known scar upon his left hand, his identity is fully substantiated.

His (William's) appearance was, of course, unique. His long bushy hair hung down upon his shoulders; he was clothed in coarse woollen garments, manufactured by himself with the rude implements used by the Indians. He had witnessed his Indian mother work with the needle, and from her had learned the use of it, which enabled him to make his

AMMI FILLEY.

The Father of the Indian Captive.

own garments; his boots were of the coarsest kind, and poorly fitted the feet which had worn moccasins in the rude wilds of the Rocky Mountains. His habits and mode of living differ materially from those who have had the privilege of enjoying the blessings of civilized life. By observation, he has treasured up many important and useful ideas. He was known and called by his tribe a medicine man, and is skilled in the preparation of medicines. He understands the secret of making steel out of iron, with the aid of a liquid. His razor is made out of a horseshoe, and is the finest steel.

He has been thousands of miles on foot and with ponies. It would be singular, indeed, if he had not learned. "To travel, is the royal road to knowledge." He has been in seventeen different Indian tribes, three of whom were savage. He speaks eleven different Indian dialects; and is a good singer in English, Spanish, and Indian.

> "I shall build a fire
> Of hickory branches dry,
> And knots of the gum-exuding pine,
> And cedar leaves and cones,
> Dry stubble shall kindle the pyre,
> And there shall the Huron die—
> Flesh, and blood, and bones!
> But first shall he know the pain
> Of a red-hot stone on the ball of his eye,
> And a red-hot spear in the spine.
> And, if he murmur a grain,
> What shouts shall rend the sky,
> To see the coward Huron flinch,
> As the Big Crows rend him, inch by inch!"

He has been where no pale-faces of the present generation are allowed to go—neither will they be, for many years to come—where scales of gold and silver ore, and various other precious metals are picked up by the Indians, with which to ornament their persons.

He has hunted down the grizzly bear and antelope, for his daily meal; has shot the California lion and buffalo for common pastime. He can give the shrill warwhoop, which can be distinctly heard for two miles; and can dance the war dance. He has with him many curiosities and specimens of valuable medicines, prepared by his own hands in caverns beneath perpetual snows, thousands of miles towards the setting sun. He has been in places in the mountains where, by looking up to the immense heights, their topmost peaks seemed to extend to the very clouds, and persons not familiar with such scenes would be frightened, and imagine the vast rocks were about to tumble upon them. He also relates many interesting incidents of Indian life and warfare, and has seen persons scalped in the most barberous manner.

> " I shall taste revenge;
> I shall dip my hands in purple gore;
> I shall wet my lips with the blood of the men
> Who overcame my braves;
> I shall tinge the lake so blue
> With the hue which it wore
> When I stood, like a mouse in a wild cat's den,
> And saw the Hurons dig the graves
> Of my brothers good and true!"

An Indian war dance is an important occurrence in their events. The whole population is assembled, and a feast prepared for all. The warriors are painted and prepared as for battle. A post is firmly planted or driven into the ground, and the singers, drummers, and other musicians are seated

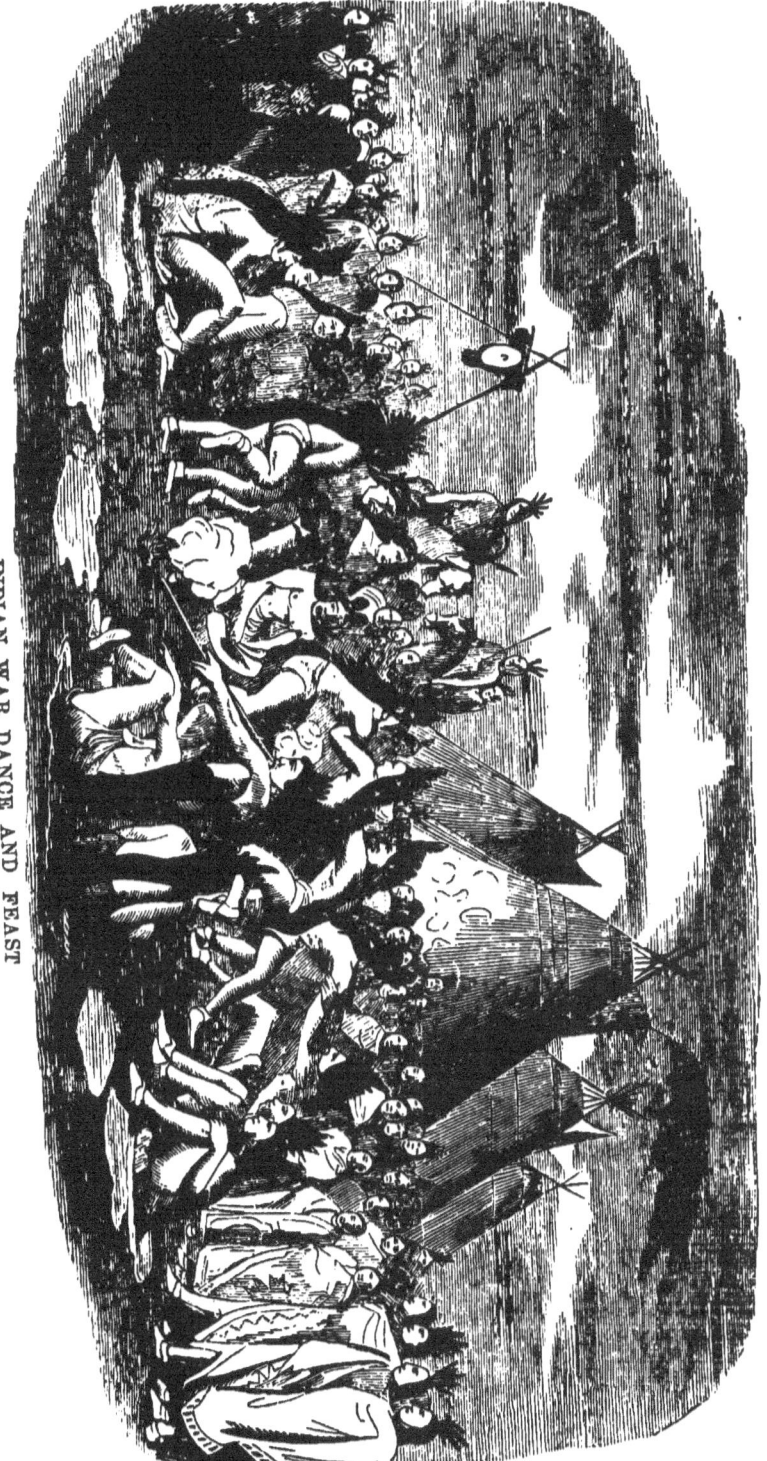

INDIAN WAR DANCE AND FEAST

within the circle formed by the dancers and spectators. The music and dancers begin. The warriors exert themselves with great energy; every muscle is in action; and there is the perfect concord between the music and their movements. They brandish their weapons with such apparent fury that fatal accidents seem unavoidable. Presently, a warrior leaves the circle, and, with his tomahawk, strikes the post. The music and dancing cease, and profound silence ensues.

He then recounts, with a loud voice, his military achievements; he describes the battles he has fought, the prisoners he has captured, the scalps he has taken; he points to his scars, personal injuries, and trophies. He accompanies his harangue with actual representations of his exploits and adventures, with man and brute, in the most eloquent manner, and to the extent of his native oratory; but uses no exaggeration or misrepresentation. It would be infamous for a warrior to boast of deeds that he never performed. If such an attempt were made, which seldom occurs, he would merit all the indignities of his nation, as the conduct of every warrior is well known. Shouts of approbation and applause accompany the narration, proportioned in duration and intensity to the interest it excites. Then all join in the circle, and the war dance proceeds until it is interrupted by a similar transaction.

In the poem "Ontwa," a scene is so well described, that we cannot resist the temptation to transfer it to our own pages. Of all who have attempted to embody in song the living manners of the Indian, the anonymous author of this poem has been the most succesful. His characters, traditions, and descriptions delineate the spirit and bearing of life. The work is not less true to nature than to poetry:

" A hundred warriors now advance,
 All dressed and painted for the dance ;
 And sounding club and hollow skin,
 A slow and measured time begin.
 With rigid limbs and sliding foot,
 And murmurs low the time to suit,
 Forever varying with the sound,
 The circling band moves round and round.
 Now, slowly rise the swelling notes,
 When every crest more lively floats ;
 Now, toss'd on high, with gesture proud ;
 Then lowly, 'mid the circle bowed ;
 While clanging arms grow louder still,
 And ev'ry voice becomes more shrill,
 Till fierce and strong the clamor grows,
 And the wild war-whoop bids its close."

We will not attempt to follow him in his peregrinations from the Northern lakes to the Gulf of Mexico, and from the golden domes, silver sierras, and verdant valleys of the Montezumas back into the rugged cliffs and deep gorges of the Rocky Mountains, where the rocks rise in triumphant grandeur many thousand feet above, shelving nearly across the chasms, covered with snow and glittering ice, where the effulgent sun never shines ; and onward, further west, through the lovely Willamette Valley, down the banks of the Columbia, from its source to its entrance into the placid ocean, and around the inexhaustible forests of fir and Lebanon cedar, and untold mineral wealth ; where the king of birds, with huge proportions, spreads his broad and potent pinions from the golden rocks of the mountains, and builds his nest, to the lofty branches of the red wood, above the sound and roar of the cataract ; where there is material wealth for future greatness, with an Oriental climate.

Dazzling as has been the career of the El Dorado of our day, and glittering as is the shield of the Golden State in the eyes of a wonder-stricken world, yet must her destiny grow dim before the rising star in the West—Oregon—that will sparkle in the galaxy of the Republic and make many of her older sisters look to their laurels. Take it all in all, Middle Oregon is one of the finest spots of Nature.

Such have been the scenes and life of the long-lost Jackson boy, since he was stolen from the oak openings of Michigan, and crossed the broad rolling prairies of Illinois and Iowa, on to Salt Lake, and into Oregon.

We should spread the broad mantle of charity over his imperfections, for if there ever was a person entitled to our sympathy, when we take into consideration the fact that he has been isolated from parental care, he is one. Thus taken, he must have inevitably lost his language, and with it all distinct recollection of father, mother, home, and all that he held dear in childhood; all, save his early sufferings amid storm and exposure. Often has he experienced sad and bitter feelings, when, in the dark and solemn forest, by the solitary camp-fire on the banks of some murmuring stream, looking eastward towards the rising sun and over the lofty heights which divide the waters of the Pacific from those of the Atlantic, with no bed but the cold ground, no cover but the broad canopy of heaven, he contemplated the long journey between him and the place of his nativity.

He returns and proves his identity; claims his birthright; and, in his own peculiar style, in the following pages, presents to the public his autobiography; thus removing the withering blight of suspicion which has hung like a cloud over the girl and family, whose misfortune it was to have charge of him on that memorable 3d of August, 1837.

3

It is necessary that we should say something in relation to Mary Mount, the girl who had the boy in charge on the day he was stolen by the Indians. As related elsewhere, she, on the non-discovery of the lost boy, at once became the object of suspicion, and her subsequent life must have been indeed intolerable. Suffering under the imputation of having committed a horrible crime, and no legal proceedings having been instituted to prove either her guilt or innocence, she was a marked person in the neighborhood. Her every appearance elicitod such remarks as: "There is the girl that murdered Filley's boy;" "That is Mary Mount the murderess;" "There is no possible doubt that she made away with Filley's boy;" etc. Citizens of Jackson, when visiting other parts of the State or country, were plied with all manner of questions concerning her: yet no opportunity was afforded her to legally and effectually remove the stain thus fixed upon her. In the days which have passed since the time when the boy was stolen, and which to her must have been YEARS of torture, she has become a woman of education and refinement. She married, and the suspicions which attached to her made her married life one of misery. But she is still living, and the odium which had fixed itself upon her has been removed, and she now stands forth in her true character, as an innocent, greatly injured and respected woman. The return of the long-lost boy was to her a happy event, and one which she will remember during every one of her succeeding days, which no effort will be spared by those who cast contumely upon her, to make happy. She assures us, from her intimate knowledge of the boy stolen, that the person who has now set up a claim to be that boy, is no impostor.

WILLIAM FILLEY,
The Lost Jackson Boy and Indian Captive

LIFE AND ADVENTURES

OF

WILLIAM FILLEY.

———•———

CHAPTER I.

Apology—Early recollections and treatment—First information as to his nativity—Return—Selection of James Z. Ballard to edit this book—Camping-
ground of the Indians near Fort Kearney—Indian Habits—The warlike and
blood-thirsty Siouxs—Burning of a pappoose—A squaw experiments on a pappoose with boiling water—Horrible cruelty—The death penalty.

JACKSON, MICHIGAN, October 1866.

This narrative, containing some of the outlines of my event-
ful life, is written in much hurry, as I have many friends and
relatives yet to visit in this State as well as in the States of
Illinois, New York and New England, and I am anxious to
see them.

In writing, I shall rely upon my memory. Were I alone,
with less confusion, I could do much better. Since I arrived
in this place, I have been with my father and friends to see
the old home, the swamp, the lake, the place in the woods
from whence I was stolen, and have had the old Indian trail
pointed out by my father; and, together, we wept over the
grave of my mother.

All have been very kind to me, strangers as well as friends,
freely giving me money and clothes, and I have often been

invited to the homes of the early settlers. The public halls in the city have been offered me, in which to receive the friends who might wish to see me, but I had rather see them less publicly. I am often passed free on the cars, and my friends have horses and carriages which I have been welcome to use.

The readers of this work may think it strange that I have stated no date of month, spring, summer nor fall, nor the date of the year. Will you look over this, as I never stored enough of the circumstances in my mind to let me state dates, and as to paper, pens, and ink, I had not the chance to get them at all times, and moreover, never expected to come and live among pale-face whites, so you must excuse my imperfection of memory. Many people in my situation, would not, perhaps, remember as much of the customs of the many tribes as I do now, though some may think that one might have committed to memory the whole of the scenes that I have passed through in these long twenty-nine years. The first eight years of my captivity, I never saw a pale-face, nor heard a single word of English spoken. This much is a blank in the history of my life.

From the first of my remembrance, the Indians used me perfectly well in every respect; even if, at any time, I wanted any valuable article that they prized highly, each and all of them would let me have it. In regard to food, I had the best there was; and as to the moccasins I used to wear, if there was any part about them that I did not like, they would always give me the strongest they had. I was used by the different tribes that I was in, altogether better than any of the Indians used themselves. When the Indians steal any male white child, they always treat him unaccountably well, in order that he may have the due respect for them they wish to have shown them; although they do not look for much respect from a child, neither do they look for much from their children. They will correct white children in the same manner they do their own, but not by whipping. I will state hereafter the punishment of their children.

When I gained the good news that I was taken from the State of Michigan, I resolved the earliest opportunity, to come to this State, in order to try and find my relations, if I had any living here or elsewhere. I visited my own tribe in the fall of the same year, which was 1860. When I came to tell the story to the head Chief, and the Council, and the rest of the tribe, they all told me that they should not advise me to go, but would freely give me the privilege to use my own mind on the subject, besides, they were more inclined for me to leave the tribe on so important business than to stay with them and never know whether I had any relations or not. I had made up my mind in the fall of 1865 to leave the next spring.

I left the Camanche tribe on the second Monday of last March, 1866, and I had a party of my tribe as a scout, and also to protect me from all danger through the mountains, until I reached a party that were crossing the Plains for the East. Since I arrived here I have seen something over four hundred old settlers who knew of the circumstances of my being lost on the third day of August, 1837, and the greater part of the number were in search of me at that time ; and nearly every one of these old settlers have talked with me about writing my life to the best my memory would afford. I have concluded to try it, but I am not accustomed to write in this manner my readers must not find fault with me if I don't place every word in its proper order, and more especially as I have been deprived of the privileges which the pale-faces enjoy. My father, Ammi Filley, told me that my brother-in-law, James Z. Ballard, would be as good a person as I could get to assist me, in Jackson or elsewhere. And, on gaining this information from my father, I resolved to have no other one have anything to do with it, in any way whatever. What James Z. Ballard has written in regard to the time and the circumstances of the case, when I was lost, is worded a great deal better than I can write.

Below Fort Kearney, on the River Platte, say two hundred miles, is the first place of my recollection, and of that I remember but little. The Indians here used to have their winter quarters at different points, sometimes at one place, and sometimes at another. The living here was generally on buffalo and deer. The habits of this tribe differs from all other tribes, except savages. They eat food with fingers, and lie on the ground, mostly. In fall, hunt meat for winter, and jerk to keep sweet. After fall, lay idle until spring, or early spring. Then the summer would be spent in ranging and fishing. Don't recollect of any reptiles except the hoop-snake and black viper, of which the bite is instant death. Stayed with this tribe until I was about nine years old, then left to the Sioux tribe, who are warlike and bloodthirsty, fear forming no part of their nature. They live much as the tribe first mentioned, except they catch beaver and eat their hind-quarters, and catch mecunis. This must be what they call the muskrat in this part of the country. They generally kill their game with the bow and arrow.

The Sioux are very cruel to those against whom they entertain revengeful feelings; and are, also, in most cases, cruel to their horses if they don't do as they wish them to. The squaws, as a general thing, do all the drudgery or work. They marry by the moon or summer, as it best suits the parties.

The power of the chief of this tribe is greater than of any tribe with which I am acquainted. He governs the councils strictly to the letter in every respect. Crimes are not punished so severely as in some other tribes with which I have been; although, in some harsh cases of burning pappooses, starving, etc., if found guilty, the nearest relative is required to act the part of executioner. I know of one case where a squaw left her pappoose with another squaw, to take care of for a short time, while the mother went to the farther part of the camp on business of some kind. While she was gone, the squaw with whom she left the pappoose, burned it almost to a cinder, or so nearly so that there was nothing left but the upper part of the skull. The mother came back in the evening, and to her astonishment found her pappoose burned to death. She went to the chief and stated her case. He went to the wigwam to see if the statement was true, and found that it was. The old chief could not sleep that night, his mind being so troubled with the thoughts of the horrible crime which had been perpetrated. He laid until nearly midnight, when he arose and called the council together for the purpose of trying the squaw who had committed the crime. The council came together and ordered a search to be made for the guilty squaw. She was found in the afternoon of the next day. When found, the council gathered together in a circle, the chief in the midst, and examined the mother. She stated her testimony several times, and swore by the Great Spirit that her statement was true. They then questioned the prisoner in regard to to the crime she had committed. She said nothing for a short time, but finally her conscience so smote her that she confessed the fact of having committed the crime. She stated that she did it to get rid of the pappoose, because it cried so much and was so troublesome to take care of. The

council deliberated over the case, and found her guilty of burning the pappoose. The sentence was that her nearest relative
should tie her to a stake and execute her, by first cutting out
her left eye, then drawing out one of her finger nails,
and then work at the other eye, and another finger or toe
nail, and so until she was dead ; all of which he did, keeping
at his bloody work until after she was dead. If this torture
should be perpetrated by white folks, it would be looked upon
as barbarous in the extreme ; but with these Indians this is
nothing, in comparison with some of their executions.

I heard of an old squaw who had the care of a small pappoose only three or four hours, but through much wanton cruelty she scalded it to death, and then put it out of sight as
well as she could. It was only a few days before the pappoose was found. The chief was made acquainted with the
facts, and went, as he was wont to do, to ascertain the truth
of the statement. The squaw who committed the crime was
then found, and her trial began ; but soon after commencing the trial the guilty squaw confessed that she scalded the
little pappoose to see how long it would live in boiling water.
She stated that she dipped it in by the hand first, then one of
the feet, then the other hand, and then the other foot, and she
concluded she had punished it about enough. She finished by
putting in the head of the pappoose until it was all covered.
The chief and the council sat and looked very sad and grim.
They were so uneasy in hearing the statement of the cruel
squaw, that the whole council were glad when she had finished telling of the plan she took to try the experiment of
seeing how much the innocent pappoose could suffer before
its heart would cease to beat. The sentence of this squaw was
to be scalded in the same manner as she did the young child.
Even then they were not satisfied, as they went to work on

her in double madness after she was dead. They began to pluck out her eyes and draw out the finger nails, as well as the toe nails. When the Indians have a case of this kind, they do not know when to stop. The pale-face would shudder at so cruel and barbarous a way to put a guilty criminal to death, even if the criminal had put his victim to a ten times more horrid death than this young pappoose suffered. But there is no shudder for the barbarous Indian. I could tell you of far more cruel cases than this, but it makes my very blood run cold when I think of the cruel death scenes I beheld while with this tribe.

CHAPTER II.

At this time, I went to the Big Crow tribe. I ought to be some fond of these Indians, as they brought me in contact with white folks; and I knew that I was a white boy, but could not understand any of the white folks' language. I knew the disadvantage of not understanding English, although I had forgot my mother tongue; but still, knowing that I was at times among white folks, and not knowing what language they spoke, it was very hard for me to make them understand what I wanted. I can remember very well how mad it made me because they could not understand me in the way I wanted them to; and not only myself, but the Big Crow Chief and tribe as well, knew the disadvantage of not understanding the white folks. If they wanted anything from the pale-face people, they would send me to get the desired article.

'About this time, was the first finding of gold in California by the whites. The Big Crow Chief and tribe, as well as the chief of the Walla Walla tribe, concluded to put me with the pale-face people, in order for me to learn and speak their language, if they had any, as it was generally thought by most all these tribes that they understood each other on the same principle as some wild tribes, that is, by signs more than words.

Soon after this, the gold flow of emigration began, in order to gain the precious yellow metal that had been seen in the far West; as some of the emigrants found the precious stuff, and, sending the accounts to their friends in the far East, they began to emigrate in a short time by hundreds.

It was not long from the beginning of the finding of gold that the emigrants began to build villages; some of these, after a short time became cities, as they were called at that time in California. But still, they increased so much that they concluded to build school houses; and, when the time came, the people of San Francisco decided to build a large and permanent school house.

A short time after this, the chief of the Big Crow tribe and the chief of the Walla Walla tribe,

> "Two mighty chiefs, one cautious, wise and old,
> One young, and strong, and terrible in fight,"

took me to this San Francisco school, and placed me with the pale-faces, in order to learn to talk with them. This was the hardest work I ever did in my life—to learn to speak English again, not knowing at that time whether I had ever spoken English or not; and I was also ignorant of the fact that I had been stolen from white folks. As near as I can recollect I remained at school in San Francisco a little over three years, but, before this time had expired, I found out to my great joy, that I had learned the language of the pale-faces, and, also, that their language was not the most of it signs and characters. I cannot tell how happy I was when I could talk to the whites and make them understand me. I can recollect, as well as if it was only yesterday, how I used to be talking to everybody, in order to find out the names of different things that I did not know anything about. I used to ask the names of things, and put them down on bits of waste paper that I would find about the streets, and sometimes on smooth bark. The reason I did this, recollect, was because I had no money to buy paper with.   This was the most trouble I had at this time; I thought more of a sheet of paper than I do of a whole quire now.   So you can form something of an idea of what a state of poverty and destitution I was in—no one to tell me when I was doing anything wrong; and, more than that, did not care whether I learned to steal or not.   But as I had to get along the best I could, I made the best I could of it, under the circumstances.

But then I had another hard thing to do, and that was, to leave the pale-faces in California, go back to the tribe, and be in bondage again.   Tongue cannot tell how sad it made me feel to know that I had got to be thrust away from my new found friends, that I had become so attached to, and to be, as I thought, almost shut out of the world again, to lead a sad, mournful, and wandering life.   Still, I had to stand it, for when the chiefs of the two tribes that had sent me to school came for me I had to go, without making any fuss about it.   Had I been stubborn about going with them, they would have punished me very severely, by lifting me up by both of my ears for a few seconds.   [Indians correct the white children they have stolen in the same way that they do their own, but not in quite so severe a manner.   The way is this, when a very small pappoose, say three summers, or, as the pale-faces say, three years old, does wrong, the Indians will lift it gently up by the ears, not bearing the whole weight of the body when so young; but commencing at so early an age begins to train them in the punishment principle, and does not hurt them very much, and is done to make them mind.

TAKEN BY INDIAN CHIEFS

From School in California back to bondage in the Rocky Mountains]

When they are four or five years old and require punishment, they are lifted bodily up by the ears and are told why and what it is done for, which hurts them considerably. It is not generally the case that a pappoose requires to be lifted up more than three or four times before they will mind strictly when spoken to, and by this mode of punishment they will mind other persons and Indians as well as their parents. Indians think this a much better plan than to whip them, as it makes them mind so close that a word or look is enough.] At times, it would seem to almost take my life. Pale-faces in Eastern climes might suppose that I need not dread going into bondage, as they might have supposed that I was at liberty. But that was the case, as, for the gold the two chiefs gave them for taking care of me at school, it was for them to keep me very close to them, so as not to enjoy my whole liberty. Still I was happier here than I had been in all my life.

But before I close this part of my life in California, I will tell you that I saw the chief of the Camanche tribe, and as the former chiefs that claimed me gave me the liberty to talk with him, I did so in the most earnest manner possible. I told the chief that I had been to this school for a little more than three years, and was now a tolerable good scholar in speaking English and also in writing. I thought I was a first-rate scholar when I could but fairly write my name, but I have found out the difference since. But, to go back, I told the Camanche chief that I was dissatisfied with the Big Crow and Walla Walla chiefs and tribes, and that I wanted him to get me away from them, and then I would be his prisoner and captive. He accordingly went and saw these chiefs, and made a bargain for me; but what the bargain was I never knew, as the Camanche would never tell me. But this much he told me, that I must go with these two chiefs into what is called New Oregon, and stay until the next spring, it being late in the fall when I saw him. I went back with them in a happier mood, knowing, as I had been told, that I could get with the Camanche chief, and would soon have my liberty.

The next four months seemed the longest time of my existence; the time wore away very slow to me, yet not without hope.

CHAPTER III.

The transfer effected—Adoption—Made a Chief and head Medicine man—Liberty—Surmises concerning relatives—Occupation as second Chief—Inability of the Indians to understand English—Friendship and love of the Indians—How to jerk meat—Panther hunting and its dangers—Torture of panther whelps—A panther fight—Distressing situation—Relieved by three pale-faces, escaped prisoners from the Osage Indians—Take pale-faces to my tribe, who kindly treat them and suffer them to go on their way—The Osage Indians—Their manners and customs—Their cruelty—Tortures—Roasting a pappose—Religion of the Osages.

The spring came, and, to my great joy, with it came the Camanche chief. The moment I saw my protector, as I was told he would be, I sprang towards him as quick as a panther would leap on a deer. This chief I found to be my friend, indeed, although, for about a year, he and the tribe used to watch me very closely. Soon after this, I was adopted into this tribe, and chose to be their chief, but not the head chief; I was next to him in rank. At this time I had my first liberty. How does the reader suppose I felt at my being almost as free as the deer or the antelope, to stay or go when I wished? If I was ever happy in my life, I was at this time. It seemed so strange to me, when I had no one to watch me, I would sometimes sing and dance, and be almost at my wit's end, to express my happiness.

I used to often wonder to myself wether I had a white father or mother, or any sisters and brothers whom I did not know. Thousands of times I thought of this, but still, at this

time, and for years to come I was left in the dark, as to whether
I had any pale-faces for relations.   I never, at any time,
thouhgt that my father was an Indian, or my mother a squaw.

Some time after being chosen chief in my tribe, I went on
a hunt, in company with four Indians, for the smaller kind of
antelope.   Our range was near the Blue Ridge Mountains, a
portion of the country seldom visited by panthers, they
generally being found much farther to the south.   On this
occasion, we came across a very large panther, with two cubs.
These cubs we caught; and, without any thought of the
danger into which we were running, we commenced teasing
them for amusement.   We cropped their ears and tails, which
set them screaming, and then we stuffed their mouths with
jerked bear meat to stop their screeches, which were enough
to make you tremble.   It was fun to see the savage young
brutes attempt to get at us, but we kept them off with burning
pitch-pine knots.   Their cries soon brought several full-grown
male and female panthers to the scene, and then our danger
began.   Having no horses, we could not get away; and everything seemed to be against us.   We managed to keep them
off by firing charges of small shot into them, which made them
only the more savage.   Our danger becoming greater every
moment, four of us succeeded in reaching a ledge of rocks
some one hundred feet above the infuriated panthers, but the
fifth was seized by four of the animals and instantly torn to
pieces.   The taste of blood, thus obtained, made them more
ferocious than ever, and by the time we were safely on the
ledge of rocks mentioned, we found the panthers had reached
an equal height, and were about to attack us from both sides.
With no means of escape, our only hope was to fight
them to death.   With our rifles and other weapons we
commenced the conflict, and after several hours' severe fight

the last of the panthers was driven off from the ledge, leaving but two of our party, two others having fallen in the fight. As it would be dangerous for us to remain, we climbed up to a higher ledge of rocks, where we laid down to sleep, both being entirely exhausted in the deadly struggle through which we had passed. On awaking in the morning, I found my only remaining companion dead, the wounds he received in the fight with the panthers having proved fatal. My situation was then very distressing; having been without food or water for two days and three nights, I was very weak and unable to reach the plain which stretched away for miles below me. As if by a special act of Providence, I heard a gun fired, and at once answered it by firing off my own rifle. I soon discovered that the first report of a gun was a party of three white men, and with their assistance succeeded in reaching the level plain. These white men were escaped prisoners from the Osage tribe of Indians on the south fork of the Platte River, where they were encamped for the season, having been with them three years, and had then been wandering thirty-three days in the various ranges in search of the route to Great Salt Lake City, having become bewildered. At the time we met they were several degrees out of their way, and I took them with me to my tribe. They were kindly treated by the chief and council, after remaining some time they were permitted to go on their way towards their friends, well provided with everything they wanted.

While stopping with my tribe, these pale-faces told me many things concerning the manners and customs of the Osage Indians with whom they had been prisoners. These Indians were very cruel and bloodthirsty, taking great pleasure in putting to death the pale-face squaws and children who

4

fell into their hands, first torturing them in the most fiendish manner. One case they stated was of a pale face pappoose, an infant at the breast, which they tortured to death in the following manner: They bored holes in its ears, and running wampum belt strings through the holes, danced it up and down by these strings until it was dead. When they found the child was dead, they danced the Indian death dance around it, and then proceeded to roast it by a slow fire, as they said, to purify the spirit so that it would be received into the Indian's happy land.

There is little civilization among the Osage Indians; yet they believe that in the happy hunting grounds they will enjoy greater privileges than other tribes of Indians. One of their happy ideas is, that every Osage Indian who reaches that happy land will have three squaws for wives; and the squaws believe they will have three husbands. They also believe they will live in the happy hunting grounds until the land turns to gold, out of which the good Indians and squaws will build a golden wigwam for the Great Spirit, who will be constantly with them; that he will fish and hunt for them, and prepare their food. In this belief they will roast a pale-face squaw to purify her for the happy land where they are to live, that she may cook for them when the Great Spirit is hunting and fishing. They inflict the most horrible torture in this operation, which is done by a very slow fire, and is continued even after death has released the victim from their fiendishness. If, while being burned alive, groans or cries escaps from the unfortunate pale-face squaw, water is poured down her throat, as the savages believe, to stop the fire from burning her up too fast. If she should die quicker than they think she ought to, she will not be fit to enter the happy hunting grounds, but will remain at the gate to wait upon all the Indians and squaws, wash their dirty feet before they enter, and gather tobacco for them. If her duties in this position are well attended to, she will, when the land turns into gold, be allowed to join them in the happy land. In the event of the Great Spirit leaving them, this pale-face squaw will have to take his place in hunting, fishing, and cooking for the good Indians and squaws. As a final reward, she is made the wife of the Great Spirit when he comes back; but if she is not a good wife, and won't spread out the bear or buffalo skin for the Great Spirit to sleep upon, she is sent out among the bad Indians, where they have to do all the hard work in tanning the skins and making moccasins for the good Indians.

My business as under, or second chief, of the Camanches, was to do all the trading that the tribe wanted done. It made no difference how small the pelt was, nor how simple the article, if any of the Indians had any such to trade, it was my place to try and sell it for him, and make as much as I could. I did this to get acquainted with this strange tribe, as you must know that I could not get acquainted with them all in one year, for there was a large number of them. The tribe were naturally fond of me, more so than they would be of other pale-faces who do not live among them.

When I knew that the whole tribe took a liking to me, (and this I knew by the treatment I received from them), and that they liked me as much as it was possible for them to love a white chief, and looked upon me as their guardian, protector, and friend, then, and not till then, did I begin to learn something for my future benefit. In such a case, should one ever turn his mind to go and live among the pale-faces, or to be their chief medicine man, they will make him what you would call their chief or prominent doctor; they will learn him all the plants and barks they use in their treatment of different complaints, both external and internal; he will have the chance to learn how to prepare all their medicines, and everything they know which will be of any advantage to them. Now, the reader must be well aware that such a tribe of Indians have all the fondness for this pale face chief that they can possibly have. The chief is called upon, when he has learned all I have above stated, for any case of consequence. He is above all the rest of the medicine men, in preparing and dealing out the different classes of medicine. It matters not what the case may be, he is called upon to superintend. This is the most lofty grade in which such an one can be stationed amongst Indians. He also oversees all the meat that is caught by them to save for the next year's food; he has the regulating of all meat that is jerked. There are probably thousands of the whites who do not understand the manner of jerking meat. There are various ways of doing it, and I will state to you one of them.

First, select a spot that is considerably on a descent; then go up from the level ground, say twelve or sixteen feet, and dig a square pit six or eight feet deep. When you have done this, dig a trench from this square pit, say eighteen inches wide, until you run out on level ground; then you will cover this trench over with stones, and grass turf on the top of them, and dirt on top of the turf. This forms a flue. Your meat you will cut in moderately thin slices, and use twine or bark in order to hang the meat on a short stick: put one end of this stick in the ground, so that it will be firm and not slip; string the meat on this stick, so that it will not touch the ground, and close together, only not to touch; then place your sticks with the meat on, one above the other, until you have all your meat in the pit; then get some very strong sticks or poles and lay a number of them across the pit: then stretch a hard hide quite tight over the top of these poles, and put some earth over this hide, until you have completely covered it. Well done. Build a fire with dry wood in the mouth of the flue, and the smoke will reach the pit. This warm smoke will fill the pit and warm the sides, so that it will cause a damp, gassy vapor to arise from the bottom and sides. This vapor, if kept going for twelve or eighteen hours, takes away or destroys the animal life. This meat, if covered close enough to keep all flies from it, will keep as well ten years as it will two. Fresh meat, in a temperate climate, if hoisted up forty or fifty feet, will keep perfectly sweet in the summer time from four to six weeks. The reason is, because we are so near the Pacific coast, and get the salt sea-breeze; and, besides, being in a temperate clime, the atmosphere is more regular, and less changeable, by far, there, than in this State. I have wandered now, from one thing to another, till I have got back to the State of Michigan.

CHAPTER IV.

I will now go back to the Rocky Mountains, which is the spot where the Camanche tribe mostly ranges in the fall and winter seasons. We do but little in the winter—our pastime, generally, is to practice with the rifle, tomahawk, and knife; play different games that we are accustomed to; read, and play the fool with each other. But the Indians are not like the pale-faces, they are not so quick tempered with each other.

Our marriages are arranged in a somewhat peculiar manner. I will state this particular as modestly as I can: They will marry by the moon, or summer, or for a longer time. But, say that the Indian marries for a moon (this is what the reader would call ·a month), then, if the squaw becomes pregnant, they are married for life; then they may fight, bite, scratch, kick, wrangle, and quarrel with each other as much as they have a mind to. But if they finally separate, so as not to live together for two moons, they are separated for life, and neither the squaw nor Indian can live together again; and, besides, if the squaw is caught with this Indian or with another Indian, or the Indian with another squaw, they are tried by the chief and council, and, if found guilty, are sentenced to the penalty of death. So much for the Indians and squaws. You may think it very strange, but I have seen, in my tribe, some Indians and squaws as pale-faced as any of the whites. But, although this is the case, these are of pure Indian blood. A pale-face will not be used very civil if he undertakes to persuade one of the squaws of my tribe to marry; he would get punished very severely, as such conduct is a thing that will not be allowed in our tribe. If he goes beyond our laws, then we will try him, and, if we find him guilty, then we will punish him in such a way that he won't try that plan again as long as he lives.

Some of our tribe can speak the English language much better than I can. Many of them cannot speak it at all. This part of our tribe are indolent, and don't care whether they learn anything for their benefit or not. It would be greatly to their benefit if they could speak English, as they would then have a chance to learn the manners and customs of the whites.

This tribe dresses far different from any other tribe. Most of the other tribes wear only blankets and skins, and a breechclout; our tribe wear pantaloons, somewhat in the shape of those worn by white men, but the coat is shorter, reaching not much below the hips. The squaws wear under and over-clothes, in much similar shape to the white women. The first dress worn in my tribe was worn by the squaw of the head chief, or what the reader would call *wife*. She had got a dress pattern from a white woman in the Willammette Valley, State of Oregon. The chief squaw cut out the dress. I was in the cabin when she first put it on; I did not like it, as it only came down to her knees. I cut this dress from off her body. Then I persuaded her to let me cut one out for her, by the pattern she had got; she did it, and I cut it to reach

down to her ankles and persuaded her to wear it.   I liked the
shape of it much better than the one she had made for herself.
I may say, that it was not over three years before every squaw
in the tribe had dresses, and made them as long as the first
long dress I cut.   It was through my means that the squaws
in my tribe were persuaded to wear dresses at all; neither did
the Indians wear pantaloons or jackets, until I induced them
to do it for their comfort, decency, and happiness.   Now, the
Indians or squaws are not ashamed to see pale-face men or
women, and look them in the face.   I have done this much,
and would like to do more for them ; but perhaps I never
shall.

My readers would like to know where my tribe's camping-
grounds lay.   Our village covers quite a large space of ground,
something over eight miles square.   But this is guess work,
for there never was a chain run through there, and may not
be for several generations to come.   It is in the Rocky Mountains, and is no farming country.   The reader may now ask,
where was our trading point or post.   It was mostly at Astoria; this lays very near the mouth of the river.   Our camp
lies, as near as I can tell, from 170 to 220 miles nearly in a
north-west direction from this Astoria, which is a small town,
inhabited mostly by Spaniards, with a few American families.
We go down to this spot once a year, in order to buy tea,
flour, and powder; lead we have plenty of in the mountains.
Near Astoria,we find, in places, the natural wild tobacco.   It
is not much larger than the common narrow yellow dock,
which grows in the State of Michigan ; but it is very strong,
especially if we let it alone until it gets ripe ; it is the strongest tobacco I ever saw of any kind.   This is real tobacco, and
not what is called "Indian's tobacco," or lobelia.

This Camanche tribe is what we call a brother tribe to the

Camanches that range generally in the State of Texas. But those Camanches are a very warlike and bloodthirsty tribe.

Among the different Indian tribes who roam over the wide prairies of the far West are the Arrapahoes. They are the most crafty, cruel, and revengeful of any of the tribes with which I had any acquaintance. They are keenly alive to insult, and the death of the person giving the insult is the only satisfaction ever taken. They do no torture before killing in cases of insult, but strike deep and sure at the first chance. They permit no violation of their laws; particularly of that which forbids the enticing away of their squaws. When a pale-face is guilty of breaking this law, if captured, he is compelled to endure the most intense misery, inflicted in the following manner: They first tie the hands behind the back and tie the feet together, then they lay the victim on his back, and with red-hot flints burn some particular spot of the body, and they will continue to work at that part until it is burned to the bone. They burn off the hair, and burn the tongue and ears; then, for a rest they will drive sharp sticks under the finger and toe-nails, draw out the nails, one at a time, and then resort again to the scorching with hot flints. Should the victim be alive after all this, they will place him upon a pile of thorns, and leave him, that he may die in peace, as they say. They have an idea that the victims of this torture sometimes come to life again and practice all kinds of mischief upon them. In order to prevent this, when they bury the body, they lay it on the face, that in digging to get out it will dig deeper, and they bind the body down with long sticks, in such a manner that if laid on the back and should come to life they never could get out. They think when any one so tortured to death comes to life again that they destroy the fish in the lakes and streams and the game in their hunting grounds.

I once had one of these savages come and tell me that one of the pale-faces he had tortured to death had come to life and had been into his wigwam, bent his bow the wrong way so that it would not shoot, and drove his squaw away. I tried to make him believe that some of his Indian enimies had done it, but he would not, and remained under the superstition that he had been the victim of a visit from the ghost of the murdered pale-face. The Arrapahoes are much more superstitious than many other tribes, and no manner of argument can change them in any way.

There may be many pale-faces who don't know what a savage Indian is. I will describe them, and their tempers and positions, as well as I can, although I have stated elsewhere that I have been amongst them before. But it is impossible to describe their true character. All I know of these two strange tribes I learned by being with them two different nights. In describing one I describe both.

CHAPTER V.

We were out for a stroll, eleven years ago last summer,
(1866,) and we came across some of these savage tribes. They
took particular notice of what direction we came. I suppose
it was nearly night when we reached their camp, and they
made signs for us to stay with them for the night, which we
were very glad to accept of, as we knew that we were some
distance from water. If it had not been for that, we would
not have made any halt at all. If my memory serves me
right, we were smoking when we first went into their camp.
For a short space of time they kept a proper distance from us;
but, bye-and-bye, they drew a little closer to us, but cautiously,
for fear, as I thought, that we were going to kill them. When
they came up close to us, it was to ascertain if our mouths
were on fire or not; but when they saw us take our pipes
from our mouths and blow the smoke out, and could not see
any fire, they were greatly astonished. On smoking again,
they saw no danger, and began to be sure that we were human
beings like themselves. They would look all around us, at
our clothes, and at our silver and gold ornaments. Then they
wanted to see our guns, and their great wonderment was,
what they were for. I took my rifle, showed them some gun-
powder, and let them see me put it in the barrel; then I let

them see the rag I put on top of the powder, then took my ramrod and forced down the paper; then I showed them a ball, and let them see me put it down the mouth of the barrel, and they saw me force it down; then I took a piece of writing paper and placed it on a tree a hundred rods off, and asked them to go to the tree with me and examine it, then gave signs for them to leave the tree. When they were safe, I drew my rifle and put a ball through the paper; then made signs for them to go again to the tree, which they did, and found the ball in the tree and brought it back to me, and kept it. As near as I could make out, they understood what lead was. So you see there are some tribes so wild and ignorant that they are unacquainted with anything belonging to the pale-faces. They were very shy of us after this. They gave us some of their dried bear meat, and we partook of the same kind of bed that they did, and that was the ground, with the canopy of heaven for a shelter. In the morning we were up before they were, and they gave us some kind of meat for breakfast. I saw, that morning, an old squaw strike one of the pappooses with a stick, very hard; one of the savages then took up a good-sized club, and split the old squaw's brains out. This was enough to show me their temper, and it was well for us that we showed them what our rifles were for; had we not, we might never one of us have seen our camp-ground again.

We left soon after this, and in a few hours we saw them secreted behind some rocks, from which they attacked us with bows and arrows. If one of their arrows had entered our flesh, it is probable it would have taken our lives, for the whole flint point was poisoned, as we afterwards found out. We shot one of them at our tame antelope and he died from its effects in about two days, although it was but a slight flesh wound, I knew that the arrow must be dipped in some deadly poison, for I have thrown flint point arrows into deer and antelopes, and made very deep wounds, which would not kill them.

Panther hunting is a common pastime in the spring-time of the year. There are a great many of them at certain spots in the mountains. There is a moderately high point south-east of camp, called Range Point. A hundred and fifty miles from this Range Point, panthers are plenty, and go in groups of four and sometimes more. I have heard persons East say that the panther will follow men and women. This is not the case with our Rocky Mountain panther; as far as my knowledge goes, they never follow any one, and I ought to know, as I have ranged in these mountains for the last seventeen and a-half years. I have never been out in these ranges and came across any of them, but they have run out of my sight as if they were running for their lives. The panthers I have seen were very small, compared to the Eastern panthers which I have heard tell about. They are very hard to kill, although, sometimes, if the ball takes them at the proper spot, they may be killed very easily; I have known as many as eight or more balls to be thrown into them before they would yield up the ghost.

When we kill panthers and catamounts we always tan their pelts to make our moccasins of. The reason we use such pelts is, the deer are very scarce here in the heart of the mountains. I have never seen but very few deer in this part; what are here are on the outskirts of the mountain.

Antelope are very thick here, so numerous that it is no trouble for us to kill several in the course of an hour; their pelts are the next best pelts we can get to make a covering for our feet. I and my tribe would rather have the pelt of the moose and the elk, if we can get them, as these tan much easier than most any pelt; they are much thicker and more durable. After we tan them, we can travel over sharp stones, or even over sharp thorns, without hurting our feet in the least. This is not all. No matter how wet we get them, after they are dry they are just as soft as they were before. I can take a moccasin of our tanning, from the moose or elk pelt, and fill it with water and let it remain as long as I wish, and then no water will soak through. But it is very rare that we find any of these last mentioned animals in the heart of the mountains, though they are in the outskirts.

I always liked to range in these winding mountain valleys, on the small as well as the larger streams, as they abound in red-spotted trout. I have spent a great many lonely hours catching these small trout, merely for pastime, and then throw them away. This was the pleasantest time I ever had alone with the red men.

CHAPTER VI.

Some people here may think me very tenacious in my habits. I am, and well I might be, as I was raised, except the first five years of my life, among the red men of the mountains. I hold to just the same principles and dispositions as the red men and squaws who raised me. I am very curious and particular as to who I choose for my confidential friends in the vast community, and, more than this, I do not like to be contradicted when I know I am telling the truth. It is contrary to my principles to allow any one to dictate for me in any manner. I hold to their disposition, except that I will not allow myself to be revengeful, and kill for a very small grievance. This I would not do, and I never had enough of the red man's revenge in me to kill a human being. I have, in the course of my life, saved the life of many a pale-face, by my intercession, from scalping with the long-knife. Some folks may think that I write this last statement in order to be well spoken of. I always felt it my duty, as under chief, to do so, and, besides, it made me more friendly with the pale faces of the extreme West. It was not only much better for me, but it was a benefit to the red men I was with.

I remember, in 1857, that a small-party of white men came into our range to find gold, which they did find, and were caught by some of our Indians. They were forced to come into our camp, and were made to know that, according to our laws, they would be tried for their lives. But, by my intercession with the head chief and the council, they were given their entire liberty. Now, it is a fact, if this party of pale-faces had gone among white men, and had entered their orchards or fields and begun to help themselves to what. was growing there, they would have tried them to the utmost of their law, and, if found guilty, would have put them in the white man's prison, and kept them there some time; and if the sentence for the crime had been death, they would have tied a piece of hemp around their necks, and hung them up. Now, if I had not interceded for the above party, and they had been proved guilty, and been shot by the red men, the pale-faces would have said directly that the Indians had *murdered* them, not reflecting of the opposite case.

Again, the pale-faces think it is no sin to steal the red man's property from his land, but to steal from a white man is all wrong, and deserves punishment. I say, of a truth, they ought to be punished in the one case as well as in the other. If this were not so, there would be no honesty whatever. Some may think I am writing very sharp on this subject, but I write the truth. I have known it this way often in Oregon and California, and I do not know as there is much difference in the laws there and in the East. I am not going to hold the Indian up to the last point of honesty, for I know there are some who are not honest. But there are more honest Indians, according to their numbers, than there are whites. If this is not so, your State prisons would not be so full.

I have written the above statement from the knowledge I have gained in the States, and from the various State prison accounts of your pale-face convicts. There are many reasons why I think more of our laws than I do of yours. One is, our laws are put in full force, no matter what the offence or the nature of it. When we find any one or more of the tribe guilty, we enforce the full extent of the law against them. This is the reason we have not so many thieves and murderers in our tribe. I firmly believe, if the laws were as strictly enforced in the States as they are with us, that where ten murders or thefts are committed, there would not be more than one or two.

I have been frequently asked questions in regard to the religion professed by Indians generally. My answer has been: The Indians do not *profess* anything; they either know it or they do not know it. What I mean by this is, that what religion they have, they practice to the full extent. They don't *profess* one thing and *practice* another. Their general worship is similar to that of the Jews during the time of Moses, as we read in the Old Testament; and although they cannot get the same kind of animals for their burnt offerings as the Jews had, they use such as they have. Like the Jews, the animals they use must be without spot or blemish, and I have known them to kill for the space of two weeks and sometimes even longer, till they obtained the suitable one, without spot or blemish, for their burnt offering. Every new moon is the occasion for offering up their sacrifices in atonement for the sins committed from time to time since their last offering. They believe in a Great Spirit, who has absolute power for good or evil; but of Christianity they have no more idea than they have of the Greek language. No such word as *virgin* is known among them, and it will be difficult to make them

5

understand the *atonement*. The Camanche Indians appeal
directly to the Sun and the Earth: the Sun as the great
source of life, and the Earth as the producer and receptacle
of all that contributes to sustain them. Their sacrifices and
offerings are all made to the Sun and Earth. In their religious
ceremonies they have many chants, of which the following
are examples:

> Och auw naun na wau,
> Och auw naun na wau,
> Och auw naun na wau,
> Och auw naun na wau,
> Heh! heh! hoh! heh!

TRANSLATION:

I am the living body of the Great Spirit above,
(The Great Spirit, the ever-living Spirit above,)
The living body of the Great Spirit,
(Whom all must heed.)

> [The chorus is untranslatable.]
> Wish e mon dau kwuh
> Wish e mon dav kwuh
> Ne maun was sa hah kee
> Ne maun was sa hah kee
> Wey! ho! ho! ho! ho!

TRANSLATION:

I am the Great Spirit of the sky,
The overshadowing power,
I illumine the earth,
I illumine the heaven.

> [Slow, hollow, and peculiar chorus.]

I have only given in the foregoing the experience I had

among the Camanch tribe; other tribes vary greatly from this, of which I shall speak elsewhere.

I have heard a great many large stories told here concerning the big timber west of the Rocky Mountains; and some have told me that they have heard travelers who had been to California tell of the large red wood timber being from twenty to thirty-five feet in diameter. This class of persons may have seen such large trees, but I never have; and I ought to know, if anybody, for I have ranged all through Upper and Lower California, before there was any gold thought of. I don't remember that I ever saw one of these trees over from twelve to fifteen feet in diameter; and this is considered a large tree in this country.

From the beginning of this book, I did not intend to relate any long stories on this point beyond the truth; neither do you want to read long yarns that are all falsehood. I want to do honestly with every human being, and I had rather cut off my hand that I write with, than to tell what I know to be a wilful, absolute lie.

CHAPTER VII.

In the latter part of July, 1853, I went out for another of
my strolls. This was the warmest time I ever saw or felt.
I roamed away from one place to another until night overtook
me. I found a lodge for the night, in this vast wilderness,
under a very broad ledge of rocks, which projected over the
ground some five or seven feet. This ledge ran nearly north
and south. Here I concluded to stay for the night. I examined my rifle, to know that it was all right, and also my small
arms; whenever I was out alone in this way I always did so. I
ate what little I had with me, and then lay me down to sleep,
hoping that it would be my everlasting sleep. When I had
lain there some time, I though I saw a bright light in the
distance, directly south of where I lay. I kept a steady gaze
on this light. After a while it grew much brighter, and before long it seemed to be most as bright as day. This seemed
very unaccountable to me, as in all my ranges I never saw
such a strange light before. I raised up to go and ascertain
what the cause of this singular light could be. I started off
in the direction where it was the brightest, and suppose I
traveled some three or four miles, when I came to a spot
where, in looking off, it loooked like a large sheet of water.
This I thought very singular, as I never had seen so large a
lake in the mountains. Wondering what all this could mean,
I concluded not to venture any farther on this route, but went
back a short space and lay me down to sleep again.

I awoke in the morning, a short time before sunrise, and went back on my last nights route. Here I saw that if I had kept on my course I should have found my everlasting sleep, which I so much desired the night before—I should have walked off a high cliff of perpendicular rock, and opposite this deep gulf was where I saw the dazzling light. If any of my readers can account for so wonderful a sight, in such a spot, I would thank them to do it.

I returned to the spot where I first stopped the night previous and wandered into the valley, where I took a southerly course until I came to this deep chasm again. I walked on till I came to some ill-shaped steps which led downwards into the cave below. I procured some dry splinters of wood, to make a torch of. I went down with my torch into the depths below, and discovered still another deeper chasm; and here, alone in the dark, a sight met me which made me shudder. It was the stiff, stark bodies of several dead Indians. I made up my mind that I would ascertain the cause of their death, if possible. I went to procure some pitch-pine knots, and got into another difficulty in obtaining them; I unluckily walked on top of a mineral spring, and, before I was aware of it, broke through and fell, for aught I know, from twenty to thirty feet. When I reached bottom, I was nearly blind from the strong mineral which got into my eyes. It was with difficulty that I clambered out of my perilous situation. I rubbed my eyes a long time before I could see. After drying myself, I gathered up my pine knots and went back to the cave; I proceeded down the rugged steps and reached the place of the dead, and found, to my sorrow that they were Indians of my tribe. I knew them by their clothes, and the make and form of their bodies. I then laid them in one heap, and covered them over in the best manner I could with sticks, bark, and dry moss.

When this was finished, I went back to my tribe, after several days' severe travel, and with a hungry stomach, and gave a statement of my discovery to the chief, in council, and reported it also to my tribe. I and the chief and council began to lay plans to explore the whole of this wild and distant cave. The next day being new moon, we did not go—it is the custom in our tribe to have a burnt offering at the time of the new moon, which is the grandest offering I have witnessed in all my travels in the wilderness of the far West.

This done, we started on our expedition for the cave. We ranged some nine days before we found the wild cavern, as we took the wrong trail. We reached the mouth of it about the middle of the ninth day, and procured some dry knots with which to broil our fresh goat's meat we had procured that afternoon. This done, we laid down to rest for the night. We rose early and ate our cold meat, and then went down into the deep, dark cave, where we discovered the poor Indians in the sleep of death. Here we remained four or five hours, and danced the solemn death dance, which is a very solemn ceremony. I never saw this danced over any Indians except those who were supposed to have starved to death. We left them here, as a suitable place, where they could rest undisturbed. We then proceeded into the cave, say from sixty to one hundred feet, when we had to come to a halt, for we saw, to our astonishment, a wide wall, about breast high, and from five to eight feet wide, and beyond this breast work was a dark gulf of great depth. As we were returning back, we saw some very handsome metal, which was pure gold; we picked up some of this, and then went out to the mouth of the cave. We went back and got more afterwards, but we did not get the half of it, as it lay loose on the ground, and in ledges of the rock.

CHAPTER VIII

Hunting the North American or California Lion—Well trained horses—Ferocity of the lions—The Indian manner of attacking them—An adventure with two of them—Severely wounded.

I went out, with four Indians of the tribe, into the bush, to hunt the North American lion. When we went on these hunts, we always went on horseback, but without bridle or saddle. Our horses are carefully trained, so well that they are perfectly under our control and ready to obey their riders; when they are spoken to, they will stop quick as lightning, · and move from right to left whenever they are made to understand it; when we want to fire, they will stand quite still if told to, or they will run quite fast if it will be of any service to us. Were they not trained, they would be of no service to us in this kind of hunting.

These lions are very savage, so much so, that let them be but a little hungry, they will attack anything they come across. For this reason, Indians dread hunting them, as they have to encounter every danger possible. We have to travel from fifty to seventy-five miles before we find any of this class. of game. They live in the bush and on the trail.

When we find them, we always halt and arrange our horses in line, with their hind parts towards the lions, for the safety of ourselves and horses. They generally range two together, and we have to be very careful, or we may be attacked and lose our lives, or be badly crippled. When we can see their heads two of us fire, and the rest are kept in reserve, in case of failure. We seldom have to fire twice; but sometimes they will not die until their heads are knocked into pomice. They are as hard to kill as the common house cat. Their skins are mostly tanned and sold to traders, who will give more for their hides than for the hides of bears, but they are not so valuable to the Indians.

The range of the North American lion is in the most rocky part of the mountains, where no animal but the wild goat lives. I have known six Indians to kill, in from five to eight days, from forty to sixty of this tribe of savage brutes.

In the year 1864, an Indian and myself were out in the country where these lions range, hunting squirrels for pastime, not knowing but the lions had all left that range. When our sport is over for the day, and we are away from camp, we always quit about 4 o'clock in the afternoon, in order to make some preparation for our night's lodging. We chose, at this time, a small cave. These caves are not generally more than from fifteen to forty feet in depth. We had selected a considerable quantity of dry knots, with which to broil some of our small game, and when we had got the fire built, a very curious sound issued from the mouth of the cave. I never heard so dismal a sound before in my life. But we were not alarmed at this, and kept on cooking our game; and, in being foolhardy, lost the broiling of our supper. What was our surprise, to see two of these fierce lions only a few feet from us, and our guns as much as ten feet from us and very near them. There we sat, in awful suspense, not knowing whether to keep still or jump for our rifles. But this Indian was very true to me, and told me he would rather lose his life than have me lose mine, as he knew the tribe would not mourn so much for him. He told me to keep still and keep my eyes fixed close on the nearest beast. No sooner had he begun to move towards the rifles, than one of the lions sprang upon him, and took off his right hand quicker and smoother than I could with an axe. He did not stop, but crawled till he reached the rifles. He had just got back to me, when the other lion sprang on him, took him in his jaws, and fairly lifted him up from the ground. This made the poor Indian yell and scream with all his might, which frightened the animal so that he let go his hold and I had time to prime my rifle. I took sight the best I could, fired, and killed the animal instantly. The poor Indian lay wounded at my feet.

But we were not through yet; the worst was yet to come: the other was the male. I loaded my rifle again, so as to have them both loaded, if I did not kill with the first shot. I fired, but did not kill, yet the lion was so amazed that he dare not attack us. I fired the second and the third shot, when the wounded animal got so enraged that he sprang at me. I raised my right foot, which he clung to till I had reloaded my rifle.* His strength had considerably subsided, but I carry the mark of his grip on the joint of my big toe till this day. I fired this charge into his mouth, which released my foot; but this did not kill him yet; he rolled over on his side, and with my last charge, I put a bullet through his heart. This finished the customer. I was then in miserable pain, but not so bad as my friend, the Indian. He told me to bind up my toe, to save my own life, and let him alone. I did bind up my toe, and then tried to comfort him as well as I could under the circumstances. I managed to stop the blood from the

---

*As this story may not be believed by some, it may be well to state that on its being doubted by the lost boy's friends, he unhesitatingly uncovered his foot, and exhibited it in a greatly mangled condition. As he will be in various parts of the country after the issue of this book, parties having a desire to know the truth of the story, can have their curiosity gratified.—J. Z. B.

stump of his arm and side and proposed to hide my rifle, and
get him to one of our fall tents, to make him more comfortable. What was my sorrow, when I had lifted him up, his
arm began to bleed most severely. Then he told me to go
back to camp as quick as possible, and let him die, for there
was nothing that could save his life.

But how could I be so hard-hearted to this poor Indian?
He had most likely been the means of saving my life. Leave
him I would not then, if it cost me my life by staying, and I
did all for him that I could in my mind think of. The day
we got hurt we had enough small game to last two days. The
third day morning we were out of food, and my foot pained
me to such a degree that I could scarcely move at all. But
was I going to let us both be hungry, even if I was in severe
pain? No, this would not do. As chance would have it, I
spied a mountain sheep, or wild goat, about one hundred and
twenty rods from me, feeding towards us; I walked, as well as
I could, to a narrow ledge of rocks, about fifty or sixty feet
from where I was, and there I lay and watched my future
game for a short time, when to my surprise, I saw two Indians
nearing me. Just as I fired the two Indians fired at the same
object, so that by the three charges being fired we got the
sheep; it was very poor in flesh, but nevertheless, it came in
good time for us. These two Indians did not belong to my
tribe, but to the Walla Walla tribe, and had been down to the
south fork of the Platte River, and the day before we saw
them had lost their range. If they had not taken our trail we
would have been in a bad condition. They relieved us some,
and they said they would go to our camp and let the tribe
know of our sufferings and perilous condition.

Five days passed away, none of our tribe had come to our
help, and I had almost made up my mind that we sould never

see the tribe again. As to my walking, that was out of the question, for upon bearing the slightest weight upon my foot it would commence bleeding.

My poor Indian died the sixth day after being wounded, I was left alone, not knowing whether there were any Indians within from forty to sixty miles of me, and I felt that I was in a very bad situation. Still I weathered it through until my foot got well enough for me to walk some, and then was obliged to walk very slowly on account of the pain being so constant and severe. I knew that to get back to my tribe I had a long journey before me, and I could not travel more than a mile and a-half a day at the utmost, so you may know why I thought I should never reach my tribe again. But the Great Spirit, who rules all things in their proper course, ordered it otherwise for me, for I had traveled only about twenty or twenty-five miles when I met four Indians of my own tribe in search of me. They had been looking around for eleven days. If ever I was thankful to the Great Spirit in my life, it was then. I had worn out my moccasins, my feet were very sore with cutting them on sharp stones, and I had not had anything to eat for nearly five days except chewing a little spruce bark, which was probably the means of keeping me alive. I was so weak I could hardly carry my rifle, and had to stop and rest very often. The second day after these four Indians found me we reached the tribe in safety. Had I not met them I should probably have starved. The scars on my foot I shall carry with me to the grave; it was a long time before my bad bite got entirely well. Thank the Great Spirit that my life was saved.

CHAPTER IX.

The grizzly bear is a very hard animal to deal with, especially if there are several of them together. I never liked hunting these animals; still I had to do it sometimes. Whenever I could get out of it I would, as it is a very rare case that one or more of the hunters do not get badly hurt, or perhaps killed. I was never in danger by these bears but once, and then I had enough of it.

We left our camp in the month of September, 1852. This was a month earlier than we go hunting animals for their skins generally. We only hunt for them once in a long time, and only when such pelts are commanding a high price. We started with thirty-three or thirty-five Indians. It would have been well for many of the party if we had not started at all. When we are under good headway killing and flaying, it is our custom for some to flay, or take the pelts off, while the others keep hunting. We kept hunting until we found we were out of our range. This we knew by not seeing any regulae Indian trails. What trails there were, had been made by these bears, panthers, and other wild animals. On searching back for Indian trails, we passed a cave of considerable size, where we concluded to stay for the night. We broiled our meat, ate our supper, and made some torches with dry splinters of wood which we had collected for this purpose. When we had lighted them we started for the mouth of this large cave, entered, and walked perhaps fifty feet from the mouth, when we came to two turns or passages. We took the left hand one, and traveled on for eight or ten minutes. We passed several more passages, but still we were not at the farther end. We made up our minds to take the back track, but turned out from the passage we went in on, and soon found that we were wrong, and made another attempt to find the right one and get out. We walked but a very few rods when we were met by several grizzly bears. They brought us to a halt, but not long enough for us to see that our rifles were in order. An Indian and I held up our torches for the others to see to shoot, but this made a bad thing of it, as they could not shoot with any surety of killing the animals, wounding them only making them more dangerous. They moved towards us as fast as they could. One of the smaller ones seized me by clasping his paws around me, my face towards him. I had the presence of mind to stick to my torch and grasped one of my revolvers. Just at this instant I heard the report of a rifle, and it prove to be fired at the same bear that was loving me in a way that I did not care to be loved. This shot forced him to let go of me. This was the only bear killed that night to my knowledge. The others had gone out of our sight. We lost no time in trying to get out of this place and we succeeded, but with the loss of some blood and very sore bodies, as we were scratched to our hearts' content. After we got out we were not long in finding a ledge of rocks which overhung the ground some six to ten feet, and there we lay down to take our night's rest, and sleep, which was but little.

We wandered about in those valleys some six or seven weeks before we could find any trail that amounted to anything for our benefit. All the meat we had to live on during this time was one wild sheep and one goat, but very little water, and mineral water at that, which would make us sick every time we drank it. Finally we found a trail and traveled on it for some time; and crossing no other trails, caused us to think we were on a sheep or goat trail, as it steered very crooked most of the time. We were then out of food of every kind. In four or five days after we struck this trail we found the carcass of one of the bears we had killed and flayed as we went out with our bear company. At this time we were very hungry, and although the bear's meat smelt some and was very bad, we were very glad to cut off some and broil it and made a good feast on it. This was the hardest time I can recollect while I was with the Western Indians.

After this we reached our camp in a few days. Not one of the other Indians did we ever see again. Most likely they were all killed or starved to death.

It is no uncommon thing to see these grizzly bears in the months of May, June, July, and August ranging on the side cliffs, rocks, and ledges. Sometimes they will lie and bask in the sun, but they never do this when they are the least hungry. Often they are shot in the summer time by the Indians, merely for pastime, or to keep us in practice with our rifles. At times they will be shot as they stand or lie on the narrow ledges. Sometimes we kill them with the first shot; when this is the case they roll off and fall as heavy as though they would smash the stones on which they fall, and very often their bodies will be crushed almost into pumice. Their meat at this season of the year is not good for much, as they are generally lean and their flesh is rank and tough, not considered fit to eat by our tribe, although they are eaten by some tribes less civilized than the Camanche tribe.

CHAPTER X.

Among the tribes are some which are called, by the more advanced tribes, *dirty tribes*, because they hardly care whether their meat is clean or dirty. I have seen some of them eat frogs of any species, as well as black rattlesnakes, of which some of these tribes are very fond, and would rather eat them than any other kind of food; and many of these uncivilized tribes will suck the warm, fresh blood and would rather have it than any other liquid as a drink.

Another reason why they are called the dirty tribes is, that they never wash themselves at all. It makes no difference what kind of dirty flesh or filthy snakes they have been handling, nor what kind of nasty employment they may have been engaged in, they will not wash their hands.

There is much difference among the more civilized tribes in regard to this practice. As a regular thing they wash their hands, face, and neck every morning, noon, and night; and at other times, especially when they have been handling flesh or anything else of an unclean nature they will wash themselves in several waters, in order to be sure that their hands are perfectly free from any bad smell.

The Rocky Mountain sheep or goat are much the same, as they eat only clean, wild herbage, and drink clean water.

The timidity of these animals is very great, although it is not quite so great as that of the deer and antelope. I have heard some pale-faces here (in the State of Michigan) tell that they have seen the Rocky Mountain sheep, and also the goat, jump or leap off from ledges or rocks which were from ten to twenty feet high, seemingly for pastime or play. That much I have never seen in all the seventeen and a-half years that I was in the Rocky Mountains. But I will say that I have seen them leap many times for good reasons. I have noticed that when the grizzly bear is moving towards the sheep or goats, or has made an attempt to catch them, it is quite a common thing for them to leap off the ledges in order to save their lives. Some may ask if they do not hurt themselves in thus leaping? They will not for this reason: Their skulls and that part of their horns which is nearest the upper part of their forehead are the next thing to being as hard as the rocks that the head strikes on, so that it would be an impossibility for these sheep or goats to hurt themselves.

The wild animals of these mountains, such as the grizzly bear, North American lion, panther, catamount, lynx, wild cat, and the wolverine, are all by nature very savage, and the sheep and goats being very timid, it is natural that these beasts should be their worst enemies, except the rifle ball. The principal food of the savage animals spoken of, is the sheep, goat deer, and antelope, and they make great havoc among this class of animals.

I presume a few words concerning the climate in that portion of the Rocky Mountains where the greater portion of my Indian life was spent, will be of interest to many of the readers of this book. The climate in the mountains differs greatly from that of the valleys, the latter being warm and pleasant, with regular seasons of rain. Snow is almost unknown in the valleys; but in the mountains it is no rarity, and their peaks are in perpetual snow. A person going in summer time from the valleys into the mountains will experience a number of changes in the atmosphere. No very marked change will be noticed at the height of four hundred feet, but after reaching the height of one thousand feet the cold becomes greater at each succeeding step until, after reaching the height of several thousand feet, snow is found eternally.

As stated elsewhere, the Willammette Valley is the home of many Indians. It is a beautiful spot; plants and fruits of many kinds grow there spontaneously and in the greatest profusion. The climate is so mild that very little change of clothing is necessary, and the seasons are regular, no variable weather, such as prevails in the East and South, inconveniencing the inhabitants. It is just such a place as the Indians are fitted for, their wants being few, and work being almost a stranger to them, they are enabled to hunt and fish to their heart's content, and obtain a living without much labor.

The foregoing are some of the simple incidents and observations of my life among the Indians, written in my plain way. I confess my ignorance. Twenty-nine years of my life having been spent among the red men of the forest, of course I am much better acquainted with the Indian trails, their habits, and hunting-grounds, the wild game, and my rifle than I am with the manners and customs of the pale-faces, my own race. I can handle my gun much better than I can my pen, and I can write the simple language of the Indians much better than I can the more cultivated language of my pale-faced friends, with whom I differ in many respects. I dislike work, as I have never been taught to labor, nor brought up to do any

6

kind of business; but I am always ready and willing to help any one who is sick and suffering. This I have been accustomed to do many years. I can go into the woods and from roots and barks which I can get there (such as red cedar and other varieties) can extract oil and medicine. This my pale-face friends seldom do. I do not eat salt with my food, as I see others do at every meal. I have my butter made fresh, and use no gravy with my meat. I can get along without water or other drink. I sleep in my blanket on the floor or carpet, although it makes my friends more trouble. I never sleep on a feather bed, though my friends tell me the cold weather here will bring me to it. I shall not dispute them on this point, as I am now suffering from the effects of the climate every day, and I expect it will be worse before spring.

This is written near the home of my childhood. I thank the Great Spirit, who has been my guide in my wanderings, and who has enabled me to find my father, my brothers, and my sisters. My mother long since passed away. Oh! that she had lived, to embrace her long-lost child.

WILLIAM FILLEY,
CHIEF MEDICINE MAN, CAMANCH TRIBE,
Rocky Mountains, Oregon.

CONCLUSION.

In writing the concluding remarks to this history of the life of the Indian captive, William Filley, the author desires to call attention to the engravings embodied in the work, truth-fully delineating the features ot the lost boy as he now appears; of the boy's father, Ammi Filley ; of the girl Mary Mount, and of the different incidents in the search made when the boy's absence was first discovered. The scenes of the most important passages in the search are true to life and nature.

There has been little said in the preceding pages of the many incidents in the carrying off by the Indians of the boy. It was a subject of conversation, during many years subsequent to its occurrence, among the people of the community where the tnrilling event transpired.. It was the occasion of the death of his mother, who went down to her grave sorrowing for her first born, never being vouchsafed the slightest consolation as to whether he was dead or alive. Had his fate been known —had the faintest knowledge of the disposition made of him been known—her overpowering, absorbing sorrow, and that of his other relatives, might have been in a measure assuaged ; but the unfulfilled hope of his return broke her heart, and she died in the belief that he was no more of earth. His father wasted his strength and means in fruitless search for him, and when hope had utterly failed him, his unwearied and patient toil was rewarded by the return of his long-absent and dearly beloved boy. Nor was the sorrow for his loss confined to his parents; grand parents, brothers and sisters, uncles and aunts, and a large circle of family friends mourned him long and sincerely. Large sums of money were spent in the unavailing search, and days, weeks and months devoted to the same end. And now he returns—a man grown—is readily recognized by hundreds of those who knew him in childhood, and their hearts are made glad, for the "lost is found."

In reading these pages, it will probably occur to the reader to ask how and in what manner the Indian captive obtained intelligence of his parentage, place of birth, and the cause of his being amongst the Indians. It was in this wise: An Indian chief with whom he had had no connection or acquaintance, on his dying couch sent for him, and, under pledge of secrecy, communicated to him the fact that he was of the race of pale-faces, and had been stolen in his early childhood by the Indians, by whom he had been reared as one of their own race. This was the first intimation he had ever received from any source whatever, of his early history. From the time he received this information he was firmly determined to find the home of his boyhood, and to visit his kindred. In this he was warmly seconded by his Indian friends, who had no desire, after the many favors he had rendered them, to place the slightest obstacle in his way. The letter which he wrote to the Postmaster at Jackson, and other facts, are contained in the foregoing pages.

The author would also ask a perusal of the Indian song given in the closing pages of the book, "The Lake of the White Canoe." Mention having been made of the ability of the boy to sing in the English, Spanish, and Indian tongues, it may be well to say that this song is a great favorite with him. Its insertion in the place it occupies, is occasioned by its great length. Had it been given at the point where it rightly belongs, its length would have broken the thread of the narrative, which is now continuous.

Notwithstanding the many years that this boy was a captive among the Indians, and in the face of the many hardships through which he was compelled by them to pass, his friendship for them is of that enduring kind which time, even, cannot change or efface. The slighest insinuation against their honesty or friendship, is resented by him as a personal insult. In fact, his long residence among them, HAS MADE HIM AN INDIAN.

The subject of this narrative is at the present time visiting his friends in New England, the place of his birth, but will, previous to his contemplated return to his Indian friends, spend some time in various leading cities of the Union, not for the purpose of exhibiting himself, but to gratify the natural desire of an intelligent, searching mind in relation to the greatness of the pale-faces' country.

J. Z. BALLARD.

JACKSON, MICHIGAN.

THE LAKE OF THE WHITE CANOE.

THE SONG OF "THE LAKE OE THE WHITE CANOE."

A beautifnl poem—Sung by the Indian captivc—His favorite song.

Wo ! Wo! Wo !
Wo to the sons of the far-off land,
Weak in heart and pale in face,
Deer in battle, moose in a race,
Panthers wanting claw and tooth.
Wo to the red man, strong of hand,
Steady of purpose, lithe of limb,
Calm in the toils of the foe,
Knowing nor tears nor ruth.
Wo to them and him,
If, cast by hard fate at the midnight damp,
Or an hour of storm in the dismal swamp,
That skirts the Lake of the White Canoc!

Wo to him and them,
 If, when the night's dim lamps arc veil'd
And the Hunter's Star is hid,
And the moon has shut her lid,
For their wearied limbs the only berth
Be the cold and frosty earth,
And their flesh be burned by the gum ex-
From the cedar's poisonous stem, [hal'd
And steep'd in the blistering dew
Of the barren vine in the birchen copse,
Where rear the pines their giant tops
Above the Lake of the White Canoe!

My brother hears—'t is well—
And let him shun the spot,
The damp and dismal brake.
That skirts the shallow lake,
The brown and stagnant pool,*

* The water of the little lake (Drum-
mond's Pond) to which this tradition relates, is colored brown by the roots of the
junlper and cedar.

The dark and miry fen;
And let him never at nightfall spread
His blanket among the isles that dot
The surface of that lake;
And let my brother tell
The men of his race that the wolf hath fed
Ere now on warriors brave and true,
In the fearful Lake of the White Canoe.

Wo ! Wo ! Wo !
To him that sleeps in those dark fens!
The she-wolf will stir the brake,
And the copper-snake breathe in his ear,
And the bitterns will start by tens,
And the slender junipers shake
With the weight of the nimble bear,
And the pool resound with the cayman's
        plash.   [ash,
And the owl will hoot in the boughs of the
Where he sits so calm and cool ;
Above his head the muckawisst†
Will sing his gloomy song ;
Frogs will scold in the pool,
To see the muskrat carry along
The perch to his hairy brood ;
And coil'd at his feet the horn-snake wil.
Nor last nor least of the throng,   [hiss
The shades of the youth and maid so true,
That haunt the Lake of the White Canoe

And if he chance to sleep,
Still will his okki whisper wo,
For hideous forms will rise ;
The spirits of the swamp   [deep,
Will come from their caverns dark and

†Whip-poor-will.

Where the slimy currents flow,
With the serpent and wolf to romp,
And to whisper in the sleeper's ear
Of wo and danger near;
And mist will hide the pale, cold moon,
And the stars will seem like the sparkling
That twinkle in the prairie glades, [flies
In my brother's month of June—
Murky shades, dim, dark shades,
Shades of the cypress, pine and yew,
In the swamp of the Lake of the White
    Canoe.

Wo! Wo! Wo!
He will hear in the dead of the night—
If the bittern will stay his toot,
And the serpent will cease his hiss,
And the wolf forget his howl.
And the owl forbear his hoot,
And the plaintive muckawiss,
And his neighbor the frog. will be mute ;
A plash like the dip of a water-owl,
In the lake with mist so white ;   [view.
And two forms will float on his troubled
O'er the brake with a meteor light,
And he'll hear the words of a tender song,
Stealing like a spring-wind along,
The Lake of the White Canoe.

That song will be a song of wo,
Its burthen will be a gloomy tale ;
It will cause the rain to flow ;
It will tell of youthful love,
Fond but blighted love ;
It will tell of father's cruelty ;
It will cause the rain to flow ;
It will tell of two lovely flowers
That grew in the wilderness ;
And the mildew that touched the leaf ;
And the canker that struck the bud ;
And the lightning that wither'd the stem ;
And 't will speak of the Spirit-dove.
That summon'd them away,
Deeming them all too good and true,
For aught save to paddle a White Canoe.

It was many seasons ago,
How long I cannot tell my brother,
That this sad thing befel ;
The tale was old in the time of my father,
By whom it was told by mother's mother.
My brother hears—'tis well—
Nor may he doubt my speech ;
The red man's mind receives a tale
As snow the print of a moccasin ;
But, when he hath it once,
It abides like a footstep chisel'd in rock,
The hard and flinty rock.
The pale man writes his tales
Upon a loose and fluttering leaf,
Then gives it to the winds that sweep
Over the ocean of the mind !
The red man his on the evergreen
Of his trusty memory.*
When he of the far-off land would know
The tales of his father's day,
He unrolls the spirit-skin.†
And utters what it bids ;
The Indian pours from his memory
His song, as a brook its babbling flood
From a lofty rock into a dell,
In the pleasant summer moon.

*The memory of the Indians is as astonishing as their sagacity and penetration. They are entirely destitute of those helps which we have invented to ease our memory, or supply the want of it ; yet they are never at a loss to recall to their minds any particular circumstance with which they would impress their hearers. On some occasions, they do indeed make use of little sticks to remind them of the different subjects they have to discuss; and with ease they form a kind of local memory, and that so sure and infallible, that they will speak for a great length of time—sometimes for three or four hours, together—and display twenty different presents, each of which requires an entire discourse, without forgetting anything and even without hesitation.

† The Indians could never be brought to believe that paper was any other than a tanned skin invested with the powers of a spirit.

My brother hears.—

He hears my words—'tis well—
And let him write them down
Upon the spirit-skin,
That, when he has cross'd the lake,
The Great Salt Lake,
The lake, where the gentle spring winds
And the mighty fishes sport. [dwell
And has called his babes to his knee,
And his beauteous dove to his arms,
And has smoked in the calumet
With the friends he left behind,
And his father, and mother, and kin,
Are gather'd around his fire,
To learn what the red men say.
He may the skin unroll, and bid
His Okki this tradition read—
The parting words of the Roanoke,
And his tale of a lover and maiden true,
Who paddle the Lake in a White Canoe.

There liv'd upon the Great Arm's brink.*
In that far day,
The warlke Roanokes,
The masters of the wilds:
They warr'd on distant lands,
This valiant nation, victors everywhere;
Their shouts rung through the hollow oaks
That beetle over the Spirit Bay,†
Where the red elk comes to drink;
The frozen clime of the Hunter's Star
Rang shrill with·the shout of their bands,
And the whistle of their cress ;‡
And they fought the distant Cherokee,
The Chickasaw, and the Muscogulgee,
And the Sioux of the West.
They liv'd for nought but war, [view
Though now and then would be caught a
Of a Roanoke in a White Canoe.

* Chesapeake Bay.

† Bay of Saganaum, in Lake Huron.

‡ Cress or *crease*, a poisoned arrow,
seldom used, however, by the tribes east
of the Rocky Mountains.

Among this tribe, this valiant tribe,
Of brave and warlike Roanokes,
Were two—a youth and maid,
Who lov'd each other well,
Long and fondly lov'd,
Lov'd from the childish hour,
When, through the bosky dell,
Together they fondly roved
In quest of the little flower,
That likes to bloom in the quiet shade
Of the tall and stately oaks.
The pale-face calls it the violet—
'T is a beautiful child when its leaves are
With the morning dew, and spread [wet
To the beam of the sun, and its little head
Sinks low with the weight of the tear
That gems its pale blue eye.
Causing it to lie
Like a maiden whose heart is broke,—
Does my brother hear?

He hears my words—'t is well—
The names of this fond youth and maid
Tell who they were
For he was Annawan, the Brave,
And she Pequida, the girl of the braid,
The fairest of the fair.
Her foot was the foot of the nimble doe,
That flies from a cruel carcajou,
Deeming speed the means to save;
Her eyes were the eyes of the yellow owl,
That builds his nest by the River of Fish;
Her hair was black as the wings of the
fowl [abyss.
That drew this world from the great
Small and plump was her hand;
Small and slender her foot;
And, when she opened her lips to sing,
Ripe red lips, soft sweet lips,
Lips like the flower that the honey-bee
The birds in the grove were mute, [sips
The bittern forgot his toot,
And the owl forbore his hoot,
And the king bird set his wing,
And the woodpecker ceas'd his tap

On the hollow beech,
And the son of the loon on the neighbor-
Gave over his idle screech,   [ing strand
And fell to sleep in his mother's lap.

And she was good as fair,
This maid of the Roanokes;
She was mild as a day in spring;
Morning, noon, and night,
Young Pequida smil'd on all,
But most on one.
She smiled more sweet if he were there,
And her laugh more joyous rung,
And her step had a firmer spring,
And her eye had a keener light.
And her tongue dealt out blither jokes,
And she had more songs to spare,
And she better mocked the blue jay's cry,
When his dinner of maize was done;
And better far, when he stood in view,
Could she paddle the Lake in her White
    Canoe.

And who was he she loved?
The bravest he of the Roanokes,
A leader, before his years
Were the years of a full-grown man;
A warrior, when his strength
Was less than a warrior's need;
But, when his limbs were grown,
And he stood erect and tall,
Who could bend the sprout of the oak
Of which his bow was made ?
Who could poise his choice of spears,
To him but a little reed ?
None in all the land.
And who had a soul so warm ?
Who was so kind a .friend ? *

* Every Indian has a friend nearly of
the same age as himself, to whom he at-
taches himself by the most indissoluble
bonds Two persons thus united by one
common interest, are capable of under-
taking and hazarding everything in order
to aid and mutually succor each other ;
death itself, according to their belief, can

And who so free to lend
To the weary stranger bed and bread,
Food for his stomach, rest for his head,
As Annawan, the Roanoke,
The valiant son of the chief Red Oak ?

They liv'd from infancy together
They seem'd two sides of a sparrow's
    feather ;
Together they roam'd o'er the rocky hill,
And through the woody hollow,
And by the river brink,
And o'er the winter snows ;
And they sat for hours by the summer rill,
To watch the stag as he comes to drink,
And to see the beaver wallow ;
And when the waters froze,
They still had a sport to follow
O'er the smooth ice, for, in full view,
Lay the glassy Lake of the White Canoe.

The youth was the son of a chief,
And the maiden a warrior's daughter ;
Both were approved for deeds of blood ;

only separate them for a time ; they are
well assured of meeting again in the other
world never to part, where they are persuaded they will have the same services
from one another. Charlevoix tells of an
Indian who was a Christian, but who did
not live according to the maxims of the
gospel, and who, being threatened with
hell by a Jesuit, asked this missionary
whether he thought his friend who was
lately departed had gone into that place
of torment; the father answered him that
he had good grounds to think that the
Lord had had mercy upon him, and taken
h m to heaven. "Then I won't go to
hell, neither /" replied the Indian, and
this motive brought him to do everything
that was desired of him ; that is to say,
he would have been full as willing to go
to hell as heaven had he thought to find
his companion there. .
It is said that these friends, when they
happen to be at a distance from each
other, reciprocally invoke one another in
all dangers. The assistance they promise
each other may be surely depended upon.

Both were fearless, strong, and brave :
One was a Roanoke.
The other a captive Maqua boy,
In battle saved from slaughter*—
A single ear from a blighted sheaf,
Planted in Aragisken land ;†
And these two men were foes,
When they to manhood came,
And each had skill and strength to bend
A bow with a warrior's aim.

* The following is the practice and ceremony of adoption : A herald is sent around the village or camp, to give notice that such as have lost any relations in the late expedition are desired to attend the distribution which is about to take place. Those women who have lost their sons or husbands, are generally satisfied in the first place ; afterwards, such as have been deprived of friends of a more remote degree of consanguinity, or who choose to adopt some of the youth. The division being made, which is done as in other cases without the least dispute, those who have received any share lead them to their tents or huts, and, having unbound them, cleanse and dress their wounds, if they happen to have received any ; they then clothe them, and give them the most comfortable and refreshing food their store will afford.

While their new domestics are feeding, they endeavor to administer consolation to them ; they tell them they are redeemed from death, they now must be cheerful and happy ; and' if they serve them well, without murmuring or repining, nothing shall be wanting to make them such a-tonement for the loss of their country and friends as circumstances will allow of.

If any men are spared, they are commonly given to the widows that have lost their husbands by the hands of the enemy, should there be any such, to whom, if they happen to prove agreeable, they are soon married. The women are usually distibuted to the men, from whom they do rot fail of meeting with a favorable reception. The boys and girls are taken into the families of such as have need of them. The lot of their conquerors becomes in all things theirs.

† Virginia.

And to wield the club of massy oak
That a warrior man should wield,
And to pride themselves on a blood red
And to deem its cleanness shame, [hand,
Each claimed to lead the band,
And angry words arose,
But the warriors chose Red Oak,
Because his sire was a Roanoke.

Then fill'd the Maqua's heart with ire
And out he spoke :
'Have his deeds equal'd mine ?
Three are the scalps on his pole—*
In my smoke are nine ;
I have fought with a Cherokee ;
I have stricken a warrior's blow,
Where the waves of Ontario roll ;
I have borne my lance where he dare not
I have looked on a stunted pine [go ;
In the realms of endless frost,
And the path of the Knistenau
And the Abenaki crost.
While the Red Oak planted the land.
It was mine to lead the band.''

Then fiercely answered the rival brave,
And bitter words arose ;
Noisy boasts and taunts,
Menaces and blows,   .
These foolish men each other gave ;
And each like a panther pants
For the blood of his brother chief ;
Each himself with his war-club girds,
And forth he madly goes,
His wrath and ire to wreak ;
But the warriors interpose.
Thenceforth they met as two eagles meet,
When food for but one lies dead at their
And neither dare to be the thief ; [feet,
Each is prompt to show his ire ;
The eye of each is an eye of fire,
And trembles each hand to give

*Scalps are suspended from a pole in the lodge, and usually in the smoke.

The last and fatal blow.
And thus my brother may see them live
With the feelings that wolf-dogs know.
And when each of these brave men
Had built himself a lodge,
And each had a bird in his nest,
And each had a babe at his knee,
Their hate had no abatement known,
Still each was his brother's enemy,
And thirsted for his blood,
And when those babes had grown,
The one to be a man
In stature, years, and soul,
With a warrior's eye and brow,
And his poll a shaven poll, *
And his step as a wild colt's free,
And his voice like the winter wind,
Or the roaring of the sea ;
The other a maiden ripe,
With a woman's tender heart,
Full of soft and gentle wishes,
Sighs by day and dreams by night,
Their hostile fathers bade them roam
Together no more o'er the rocky dell,
And through the woody hollow,
And by the river brink.
And o'er the winter snows,
Nor sit for hours by the summer rill,
To watch the stag as he came to drink,
And to see the beaver wallow,
Nor when the waters froze,
Have a pleasant sport to follow,
O'er the smooth ice ; they bade them shun
Each other as the stars the sun.

What did they then—this youth and
Did they their fathers mind ?—   [maid ?
I will tell my brother.—
They met—in secret met—
'T was not in the rocky dell,
Nor in the woody hollow,
Nor by the river brink,

* Alluding to the custom of the Indian
of shaving off all the hair except the
scalp-lock.

Nor o'er the winter snows,
Nor by the summer rill,
Watching the stag as he came to drink,
And to see the beaver wallow,
That these two lovers met,
Nor when the waters froze,
Giving good sport to follow ,
But, when the sky was mild,
And the moon's pale light was veil'd,
And hushed was every breeze,
In prairie, village, and wild,
And the bittern had stayed his toot,
And the serpent had ceased his hiss,
And the woolf forgot his howl,
And the owl forbore his hoot,
And the plaintive wekolis, *
And his neighbor, the frog, were mute—
Then would my brother have heard
A plash like the dip of a water fowl,
In the lake with mist so white,
And the smooth wave roll to the bank,
And have seen the current stirr'd
By something that seem'd a White Canoe
Gliding past his troubled view.

And thus for moons they met
By night on the tranquil lake,
When darkness veils the earth ;
Nought care they for the wolf,
That stirs the brake on the bank ;
Nought that the junipers shake
With the weight of the nimble bear,
Nor that bitterns start by tens,
Nor to hear the cayman's plash,
Nor the hoot of the owl in the boughs of
Where he sat so calm and cool : [the ash,
And thus each night they met,
And thus a summer pass'd.

Autumn came at length,
With all its promised joys,
Its host of glittering stars,
Its fields of yellow corn,
Its shrill and healthful winds,

* Another name for the whip-poor-will.

Its sports of field and flood.
The buck in the grove was sleet and fat
The corn was ripe and tall ;
Grapes clustered thick on the vines ;
And the healing winds of the north
Had left their cells to breathe
On the fever'd cheeks of the Roanokes, '
And the skies were lit by brighter stars
Than light them in the time of summer
Then said the father of the maid,
"My daughter, hear—
A bird has whispered in my ear,
That, often in the midnight hour,
They who walk in the shades,
The murky shades, dim, dark, shades,
Shades of the cypress, pine, and yew,
That tower above the glassy lake,
Will see glide past their troubled view
Two forms as a meteor light,
And will note a white canoe,
Paddled along by two,
And will hear the words of a tender song,
Stealing like a spring-wind along ;
Tell me, my daughter, if either be you ?

Then down the daughter's cheek
Ran drops like the summer rain,
And thus she spoke :
Father, I love the valiant Annawan ;
Too long have we roam'd o'er the rocky
And through the woody hollow,   [dell,
And by the river brink,
And o'er the winter snows,
To tear him from my heart ;
Too long have we sat by the summer rill,
To watch the buck as he comes to drink,
And to see the beaver wallow,
To live from him apart—

My father hears."
"Thou lov'st the son of my foe,
And know'st thou not the wrongs
That foe hath heaped on me.
The nation made him chief—
Why made they him a chief?

Had his deeds equal'd mine ?
Three were the scalps on his pole—
In my smoke are nine ;
I had fought with a Cherokee ; '
I had stricken a warrior's blow,
Where the waves of Ontario roll;
I had borne my lance where he dare not
I had looked on a stunted pine   [go.
In the realms of endless frost,
And the path of the Knistenau
And the Abenaki crost.
While the Red Oak planted the land.
It was mine to lead the band."
Since then we never spoke,
Unless to utter reproach,
And bandy bitter words ;
We meet as two hungry eagles meet,
When a badger lies dead at their feet—
Each would use a spear on its foe,
Each an arrow would put to his bow,
And bid its goal be his foeman's breast.
But the warrior's interpose,
And delay the vengeance I owe.
Thou hearest my words—'t is well.

Then listen to my words :
The soul of Maqua never cools;
His ire can never be assuag'd ·
But with the smell of gore.
I thirst for the Red Oak's blood ;
I live but for revenge ;
Thou shalt not wed his son :
Choose thee a mate elsewhere,
And see ye that ye roam no more
By night o'er the rocky dell,
And through the woody hollow,
But when the sun its eyelids closes,
See that thine the example follow."

And the father of the youth
Spake thus unto his son :
" A bird has whispered in my ear,
That when the stars have gone to rest,
And the moon her eyelids hath clos'd,
Who walk beside the lake

Will see glide past their troubled view
Two forms as a meteor light,
And will note a white canoe,
Paddled along by two,
And will hear the words of a tender song,
Stealing like a spring-wind along ;
Tell me, my son, if either be you ?

Then answer'd the valiant son,
" Mine is a warrior's soul,
And mine is an arm of strength ;
I scorn to tell a lie ;
The bird has told thee true.
And, father, hear my words :
I now have come to man's estate ;
who can bend the sprout of the oak,
Of which my bow is made ?
Who can poise my choice of spears,
To me but a slender reed ?
I fain would build myself a lodge,
And take to that lodge a wife ;
And father, hear thy son—
I love the Maqua's daughter."

"Thou lov'st the daughter of my foe ;
And know'st thou not the taunts
His tongue hath heap'd on me ;
The nation made me chief,
And thence his ire arose ;
Thence came foul wrongs and blows,
And neither yet avenged.
He boasted that his fame exceeded mine :
Three, he said, were the scalps on my pole
While in his lodge were nine—
He did not tell how many I struck,
Nor spoke of my constancy,
When the Nansemonds tore my flesh,
With burning pincers tore ;
And he said he had fought with a Chero-
And had struck a warrior's blow,   [kee,
Where the waves of Ontario roll,
And had borne his lance where I dare not
And had looked on a stunted pine   [go;
In the realms of endless frost,
And the path of the Knistenau

And the Abenaki crest.
While,—bitter taunt !—cruel taunt !
And for it I'll drink his blood,
And eat him broil'd on fire—
The Red Oak planted his land,
It was his to lead the band.

"And listen further to my words—
My wrath can never be assuaged ;
Thou shalt not wed his daughter,
Choose thee a wife elsewhere ;
Choose thee one anywhere,
Save in the Maqua's lodge.
The Nansemonds have maidens fair,
With bright black eyes, and long black
And voice like the music of rills ;   [locks
The Chippewa girls of the frosty north
Have feet like the nimble antelopes,
That bound on their native hills ;
And their voice is like the dove's in spring
Take one of those doves to thy cage ;
But see no more by day or night,
The Maqua warrior's daughter."
And haughtily he turned away.

Night was abroad on the earth :
Mists were over the face of the moon,
And the stars were like the sparkling flies
That twinkle in the prairie glades,
In my brother's month of June ;
And hideous forms had risen ;
The spirits of the swamp
Had come from their caverns dark and
Where the slimy currents flow,   [deep
With the serpent and wolf to romp,
And to whisper in the sleeper's ear
Of death and danger near.

Then to the margin of the lake
A beauteous maiden came ;
Tall she was as a youthful fir,
Upon the river's bank ;
Her step was the step of the antelope ;
Her eye was the eye of the doe ;

Her hair was black as a coal-black horse :
Her hand was plump and small ;
Her foot was slender and small ;
And her voice was the voice of a rill in
Of the rill's most gentle song, [the moon.
Beautiful lips had she,
Ripe, red lips,
Lips like the flow'r that the honey-bee sips
When its head is bow'd by dew.

She stood beneath the shade
Of the dark and lofty trees,
That threw the image on the lake,
And waited long in silence there.
"Why comes he not, my Annawan,
My lover brave and true ?
He knows his maiden waits for him
Beneath the shade of the yew,
To paddle the lake in her White Canoe."
But Annawan came not;
'He has miss'd me sure," the maiden said,
"And skims the lake alone ;
Dark though it be, and the winds are high,
I'll seek my warrior there."
Then lightly to her white canoe
The fair Pequida sprung,
And is gone from the shore alone.

Loud blew the mighty winds,
The clouds were dense and black,
Thunders rolled among the hills,
Lightnings flash'd through the shades;
The spirits cried aloud
Their melancholy cries,
Cries which assail the listening ear
When danger and death are near :
Who is he that stands on the shore,
Uttering sounds of grief?
'T is Annawan, the favor'd youth,
Detain'd so long lest envious eyes
Should know wherefore at midnight hour
He seeks the lake alone.
He finds the maiden gone,
And anguish fills his soul,
And yet, perchance in childish sport,

She hides among the groves.
Loudly he calls, "My maiden fair,
Thy Annawan is here !
Where art thou maid with the coal-black
What does thy bosom fear ?   [hair ?
If thou hast hid in playful mood
In the shade of the pine, or cypress
    wood,
If the little heart that so gently heaves
Is lightly pressing a bed of leaves ;
Tell me, maiden, by thy voice
Bid thy lover's heart rejoice ;
Ope on him thy starry eyes ;
Let him clasp the in his arms,
Press thy ripe red lips to his.
Come, my fair Pequida, come !"

No answer meets the warrior's ears,
But glimmering o'er the lake appears
A solitary, twinkling light—
It seems a fire-fly lamp ;
It moves with motion quick and strange
Over the broad lake's breast.
The lover sprung to his light canoe,
And swiftly followed the meteor spark,
But the winds were high, and the clouds
He could not find the maid,   [were dark.
Nor near the glittering lamp.

He went to his father's lodge,
And laid him on the earth,
Calmly laid him down.
Words he spoke to none,
Looks bestow'd on none.
They bro't him food —he would not eat—
They brought him drink—he would not
    drink—
They brought him a spear and a bow,
And a club, and an arrowy sheaf.
And shouted the cry of war,
And prais'd him, and nam'd him a Chief,
And told how the treacherous Nanticokes
Had slain three Braves of the Roanokes ;
That a man of the tribe who never ran
Had vow'd to war on the Red Oak's son—
But he show'd no signs of wrath.

His thoughts were abroad in another path.

Sudden he sprung to his feet,
Like an arrow impell'd by a vigorous arm.
"You have dug her grave," said he,
"In a spot too cold and damp,
All too cold and damp,
For a soul so warm and true.
Where, think ye, her soul has gone?
Gone to the Lake of the Dismal Swamp,
Where all night long by a fire-fly lamp,
She paddles her White Canoe.
And thither I will go!"
And with that he took his quiver and bow,
And bade them all adieu.

And the youth returned no more;
And the maiden returned no more;
Alive none saw them more;
But oft their spirits are seen

By him who sleeps in that swamp,

When the night's dim lamps are veil'd,
And the Hunter's Star is hid,
And the moon has shut her lid,
And the she-wolf stirs the brake,
And the bitterns start by tens,
And the slender junipers shake
With the weight of the nimble bear,
And the pool resounds with the cayman's
· plash,   [ash,
And the owl sings out of the boughs of the
Where he sits so calm and cool,
And above his head the muckawiss
Sings his gloomy song,
And croak the frogs in the pool,
And he hears at his feet the horn snake's
Then often flit along   [hiss,
The shades of the youth and maid so true
That haunt the Lake of the White Canoe.